"I'm sure you'll be a great mother, and when the baby gets here, everything else will be forgotten. Everyone will see how strong and capable you are. A more than suitable leader for this modern country."

He believed everything he said because she came across as such a genuine, down-to-earth person who cared about doing the right thing. Gaia would be an amazing mom, raising a child and simultaneously running a country, defying convention and proving her place in society.

"This affects you too, Niccolo. The press think we're together. How is it going to look if we go our separate ways and I have a baby a few months down the line?"

He listened to everything she was saying, saw the picture of them so clearly in his mind it would be natural to believe there'd been a pregnancy as a result. It was easy to imagine the follow-up news article once again painting him as a villain despite his innocence on both occasions.

Movie Star Leaves Princess Heartbroken and Pregnant.

The truth didn't matter when the headline would sell millions worldwide.

Dear Reader,

I count myself very lucky to do a job I love, writing happy-ever-afters. Luckier still that Harlequin has enough faith to allow me to step into the Harlequin Romance universe. And what could be more romantic than a world where royalty and celebrity collide? That would be when a movie star goes against his no-emotional-ties rule to marry a pregnant princess in need of a husband.

One sexy dance, the whiff of another royal scandal and Niccolo Pernici stuns everyone by announcing his betrothal to the future queen, including Gaia herself.

Pregnant Princess at the Altar is my debut for the Harlequin Romance line, and I've had fun delving into the fantasy, and sometimes angst, of this new world. I hope you do too.

Happy reading!

Love,

Karin x

Pregnant Princess at the Altar

Karin Baine

Recycling programs for this product may not exist in your area.

ISBN-13: 978-1-335-59632-1

Pregnant Princess at the Altar

Copyright © 2023 by Karin Baine

Harlequin Enterprises ULC
22 Adelaide St. West, 41st Floor
Toronto, Ontario M5H 4E3, Canada
www.Harlequin.com

Printed in U.S.A.

Karin Baine lives in Northern Ireland with her husband, two sons and her out-of-control notebook collection. Her mother and her grandmother's vast collection of books inspired her love of reading and her dream of becoming a Harlequin author. Now she can tell people she has a *proper* job! You can follow Karin on Twitter @karinbaine1 or visit her website for the latest news—karinbaine.com.

Books by Karin Baine

Harlequin Medical Romance

Carey Cove Midwives

Festive Fling to Forever

Healed by Their Unexpected Family
Reunion with His Surgeon Princess
One Night with Her Italian Doc
The Surgeon and the Princess
The Nurse's Christmas Hero
Wed for Their One Night Baby
A GP to Steal His Heart
Single Dad for the Heart Doctor
Falling Again for the Surgeon

Visit the Author Profile page
at Harlequin.com for more titles.

For Mum. I wish you could be here to see
my dreams come true. xx

With thanks to my lovely editor, Charlotte,
who helped make this happen.

Praise for
Karin Baine

CHAPTER ONE

'NOT EVERY PRINCESS gets to live in a fairy tale, Gaia.'

'If anyone knows that, Mother, it's me.'

Currently her life was less handsome prince and happy-ever-after, and more unexpected pregnancy and absentee partner. Not exactly the stuff every little girl dreamed of, nor something she was brave enough to tell her family. The consequences of that particular news would be so far-reaching she couldn't face it yet.

The country of Lussureggiante—the name of which literally described the lush green land surrounding them—was a principality located near the Northern Italian border. It might be ruled by the monarchy but the inhabitants didn't always respect them. Gaia knew she wasn't going to gain them any new fans with her current status.

'I'm not sure what a movie premiere has to do with restoring the Benetti name exactly...' She trailed off, sounding more like a surly teen than a twenty-nine-year-old princess, second in line to the throne, but she had more important issues on her mind than the latest over-hyped film.

Even in the dim light of the limousine she could feel her mother's steely grey stare upon her. 'Your grandfather requests it. He wants you to be seen, so you will be accepted as the first female figurehead of the royal family when he dies.'

'No pressure, then.' There was nothing to be gained from another discussion on the subject other than causing her mother more anguish. She'd been through enough lately because of Gaia's father. He was the reason she was in this new media-focused role. The public scandal of the Prince, the future king, severing all ties with the royal family to run off with a married woman half his age had thrown the monarchy into complete disarray.

Not only had he humiliated his dutiful wife, disgraced the family name and caused their popularity to fall to an all-time low, but also now Gaia was expected to step up into his place. It wasn't something anyone had planned for, they simply had no other choice of direct descendants from her grandfather. If she wasn't put forward for the role the next in line would come from some less than desirable alternative outside the immediate Benetti family.

When she was growing up, the idea of one day leading the country had been something for her father to aspire to, not her. Therefore she'd remained mostly in the background, as the women in this family were supposed to do. Leaving the focus on her grandfather and later her father to have the hopes of a nation weighing on their shoulders. It was her duty to marry well and continue the family line. So far, she'd unfortunately endured carbon copies of her father—men who apparently couldn't commit to one woman or be content with their lot. The last no-hoper, Stefan, the vice president of a large banking firm she'd met at a garden party, had seemed a suitable match at the time. Although he would have been considered a commoner, he was descended from royalty on his Swedish mother's side. Good stock was the common perception. Until she'd discovered she was pregnant and he'd shown his true colours.

Not only had he told her he wasn't ready to settle down and have a family, but he'd later accused her of sleeping around when she told him she was keeping the baby too. It was apparent he wasn't going to be involved, and with that attitude she'd decided she didn't want him in her life any longer. A relief to him, especially when she promised not to tell anyone he was the father. They'd made a clean break, but she was still the one left to deal with the fallout.

Gaia wanted her baby. Being a daughter instead of the son and heir her father had desired, she knew what it was to be considered worthless, and would never purposely inflict that cruelty on her own child. Yes, she'd prefer her baby to be born into a warm, loving family with two parents, but she'd do her best to love enough for both parents.

A child would give her life real meaning, making her a mother, someone her child would be completely dependent on. She needed to be needed, to give and receive unconditional love she never truly believed she'd had in her life. Her mother had tried her best but Gaia knew her heart was completely devoted to her father. She'd been a disappointment to them both and probably the reason there'd been a rift between them since the beginning of their marriage.

Although she'd made the decision before her father abdicated, thinking becoming a mother would give her the purpose she didn't have in life, she wasn't going to change her mind. Even if she now had a dual role to fulfil.

She knew she was privileged to be in such a position, and she would do her utmost for her baby and her country. It simply would've been more comforting to have a supportive partner by her side.

This pregnancy hadn't happened in the best of circumstances, but she never wanted her child to feel the way she had growing up. It would be easier for her not to be pregnant for her and the family's sake, but the sheer joy she felt knowing there was a baby growing inside her was something she would not give up.

She could only imagine the joy of finally getting to meet this little one and having the privilege of raising him or her, introducing them to all the wonderful things in the world, and protecting them from the bad stuff. Being a good parent was as important to her as the other role being lined up for her future and she wasn't going to let anyone take that away from her.

Right now she was under pressure to be a good princess, deserving of the new position her grandfather was prepping her for. One which would break with family tradition in a constitution which had only revered the male members of the family, but her grandfather was resilient, if not 'modern'. With his son's behaviour so prevalent in the headlines, things had to change, and what better way to prove the family could be forward-thinking than to pass the crown on to a woman when the time came? That way the focus would be less on the rich privilege they were granted in their position, which her father had abused, and on a new enlightened monarchy granting equal rights for the men and women in the family.

For it to come out that she was on her own and pregnant would not make a good impression. She could be accused of following in her father's footsteps with loose moral behaviour when nothing could be further from the truth. All she was guilty of was picking the wrong men, like her mother.

'If you do not accept the position your grandfather is graciously bestowing upon you, the alternative is Antonio, who would surely collapse the monarchy with his disregard for tradition or decorum.'

Her distant cousin would be next in line and would be unacceptable to her grandfather and the rest of the country when he was frequently in trouble with the law. Definitely not the saviour of their reputation needed in the wake of her father's mid-life crisis.

She wasn't prepared for this new position or the expectations which came with it. Her only hope was for her grandfather to live for ever or her father to repent and be reinstated in his royal role. Neither of which was likely to happen.

So here she was, rolling up to a red-carpet

event, carrying a secret which could cause almost as much damage to the family as her father in front of the world's press.

A swell of nausea threatened to spoil her sheer white, beaded, halter-neck gown.

Even though it wasn't her fault her ex had walked away, her mother would be disappointed in her. She didn't want to imagine her grandfather's reaction when he was championing her as the saviour of the whole institution.

The car came to a stop and she could hear the crowd outside, see the throng of people lined either side of the red carpet. She swallowed down the ball of anxiety blocking her airway and threatening to suffocate her as the privacy of the car interior was about to be ripped away from her.

'Who's in this film, anyway? Anyone I would know?' With this engagement thrust upon her at the last minute she hadn't been given much information and she didn't want to go in blind. If she slipped up on a name or didn't recognise the important people tonight it would be a faux pas she wouldn't be allowed to forget.

'Niccolo Pernici. I know you like that dance film he did a while back. You were always watching it.'

Gaia blushed undercover of the semi-darkness. It was true, she'd loved the film, but she watched it for one particular sexy scene which her mother would not have approved of if she'd seen it.

'I thought he'd been cast out into the wilderness after all those rumours. Something about fraudulent business practices, wasn't it?' She'd been disappointed at the time, reading about the dodgy dealings alleged by his ex-girlfriend in the papers. It had taken the shine off her crush to think he wasn't the honourable, upstanding man he portrayed in the movies.

Yet there'd been no arrest or court case and the furore had seemed to die down after a while. He'd remained off the radar and she had imagined perhaps that he'd grown tired of this superficial world, as she had lately.

She could relate to having a supposed private life splashed all over the papers with no opportunity for comeback, advised to remain silent and dignified until things blew over.

'Apparently this is his baby and the critics have been raving about it. Which is why we want to be seen here tonight. This is his comeback, and your debut as a more prominent member of the royal family.'

'Isn't it going to look strange having two female members of the family in attendance?' Traditionally they were there merely to look pretty on the arms of the men, who were there in a position of more authority. Nothing more than clothes horses whose make-up and hair would be judged and critiqued the world over. Apparently the men added more of a sense of gravitas, or something equally sexist.

'Your grandfather isn't in good enough health to sit through these things, and your father... well, his presence is equally unlikely. Yes, it goes against tradition, but that's exactly why we should be here together. Everyone needs to get used to the idea that this will no longer be a male-dominated monarchy.' Her mother almost sounded proud of her. As if watching her daughter ascend through the ranks could erase the humiliation and shame of what her husband had done. Gaia only hoped she wasn't going to add to her mother's woes.

'Thank you for the support.' Gaia reached out and took her hand, surprised to see tears in her mother's eyes. She'd always been a rock, standing steadfast through all of her father's indiscretions, which he'd never bothered to hide, still carrying out her public duty and serving her country. All the time putting up with the emotional abuse Gaia's father had directed at her.

'You're lucky you married into this family. Without me, you're nothing,' was something she'd heard repeatedly used against her mother when objections to his behaviour were raised.

It was so ingrained in her Gaia thought it about herself too. She wasn't the longed-for male heir but a useless woman who didn't deserve her place in the family, or his time.

As far as Gaia was concerned, her mother had been the perfect princess, always acting appropriately and showing compassion for those less fortunate than herself. She could see the pain that caused her now, still having to put on a brave face when inside she was still devastated by her husband's public betrayal.

There was no more time to console her mother as their chauffeur opened the car door and the glare of cameras and lights blinded them.

As they had been taught to do, Gaia and her mother slapped on their smiles before facing the crowd.

'At what point can I leave?' Niccolo whispered to Ana, his agent, who was his plus one for the night.

'It's your premiere, Niccolo. This is Niccolo Pernici's great comeback. There will be no sneaking away.' She emphasised the last three words with a tap on his chest with her folded fan, a much-needed accessory inside the movie theatre on this balmy evening.

'You know best,' he sighed, resigned to the fact he'd spend the rest of the night smiling and posing for photographs when all he really wanted was to be alone.

'I know these past two years have been tough, Nicco, but I always believed in you. By the look of tonight's turn-out, your fans do too. All of those things Christina said about you were unproven because they weren't true. I still don't know why you didn't sue her for defamation of character after the damage she did to your reputation.'

'Because that's what she wanted—drama, attention and, most of all, a reaction from me.' His ex-girlfriend had accused him of being emotionless, a robot incapable of actual feelings. It wasn't true; he simply found life easier to get through by keeping his emotions at bay.

The death of his mother at a young age had devastated him to the point where he'd stopped talking altogether. No one had thought to tell him about the cancer which had taken her, making it more of a shock to him than anyone else when she went away for ever. It had taken a lot of therapy and counselling for him to recover, with little assistance from his father other than arranging the appointments. He hadn't wanted to talk about what had happened, just wanted his son to be 'normal' again. Niccolo's grief had consumed him and the only way he'd been able to move on and make his father happy again was to lock those feelings away. He'd been doing that ever since.

He could see why Christina had thought him cold, but the truth was he simply hadn't loved her the way she needed him to. That was what had prompted her tirade after he'd broken up with her, refusing to commit to their moving in together. She'd insinuated to anyone who would listen that he was involved in conning people out of their life savings for investments that didn't exist. In reality it was his father who mixed in some dubious business circles, always putting money before people. However, an ex scorned didn't care for trivial details such as the truth and had a ready-made audience in the press, who were all too keen to knock him off his top-billing perch. There was nothing the tabloids loved more than to build a man up, only to watch him fall back down again.

He'd been a box-office surety, thanks to his roles in crowd-pleasing romantic comedies. Then, when Christina had spread her poison, he'd suddenly found himself *persona non grata* in the industry. Offers and scripts had begun to dry up along with his chat-show requests. His refusal to take Christina to court had helped make him look guilty and cost him all of his endorsement deals, not to mention his so-called friends.

His decision to deny everyone some high-profile mud-slinging was because he didn't want to be exposed in what would've been a show trial put on for everyone's entertainment but his. There'd been a possibility the stress would've proved too much, that he would've broken down, not through guilt, but from an explosion of all the emotion he'd been fighting since the day he'd told Christina it was over. Within a few months he'd lost everything he'd ever worked for and he didn't want the world to see him broken, didn't want to let his pain win through for fear of never being able to rein it in again. It would've been a very public breakdown waiting to happen.

Instead he'd locked himself away working on his own projects, since no one seemed inclined to offer him any more work. He'd invested what money he had left, called in favours from people still willing to give him the time of day, and come up with an emotional, one-take monologue about a man coming to terms with a terminal cancer diagnosis. Based on not only his mother's last months but also his own emotional fragility at the time, it was a piece far removed from anything he'd ever done before. No one was more surprised than he when it had been lauded at film festivals by critics prior to this premiere and everything was riding on its being a success.

It was difficult to suddenly bounce back simply because the buzz around his film had made him hot property again. Especially when it had been filmed during one of the worst periods of his life. He wasn't sure he could watch himself unravelling on the big screen, all too aware it was real, raw and unflinching. No acting involved. The last time he planned on ever being that vulnerable again.

'Anyway, you should go and line up with the other subjects for our princess to cast an eye over.' Ana opened her fan with an expert flick of the wrist to rival that of any Edwardian heroine and sauntered into the screening with the rest of the crowd.

Niccolo had no choice but to fall into the greeting line. It was a royal premiere after all. His premiere. All he had to do was smile, shake hands and pray this film was a success so he could get his life back on track.

'Lovely to meet you.'

'Hello.'

'I've heard it's a wonderful film.'

He watched Princess Gaia make her way along the short line of crew who'd worked with him on the project, shaking hands and reducing them to gibbering fools. Usually he didn't put any store in their monarchy when they seemed like any other dysfunctional family, only with extra privilege and influence. However, great things were expected of this woman and he had to respect the grace with which she was dealing with the pressure. He knew what it was like to have the spotlight shining so brightly it was almost incapacitating.

As they'd been instructed to do by those more experienced in royal etiquette, he bowed and only shook hands when the Princess offered hers.

'Mr Pernici, it's an honour to meet you.'

'Likewise, Your Royal Highness.' There was no doubting her beauty, with chestnut curls falling in silken waves to her shoulders, unusual amber-coloured eyes and lips so full he imagined she was the poster girl for every red-blooded human on the planet.

He was still holding her hand, and, though it probably went against all sort of protocol, he couldn't resist lifting it to his lips for a kiss. The flash of cameras lighting up told him it was going to be a watercooler moment tomorrow, but somehow simply shaking her hand hadn't seemed enough. This was the future monarch and he might never get another chance to meet her. He'd wanted to make an impression on her and, judging by her little gasp, followed by her coy smile, he'd done just that.

'Don't you think we've dominated the headlines for long enough between us, Mr Pernici? Anyone would think you were purposely causing a scene.' She was trying to hide her smile but her eyes were blazing with amusement at the stunt he'd pulled. Maybe she liked a rebel who didn't behave exactly as he was told to do, or perhaps she was enjoying something different from the norm. Whatever it was, she clearly knew who he was and what he'd been through.

'That wasn't my intention, Ma'am, I assure you. I'd prefer it if no one else was around.'

'You and me both,' she sighed, letting that polished smile momentarily slip to give him a peek at the emotionally exhausted person behind the glamour. In that moment it seemed they'd made a connection, recognising each other's recent hardships and how much it had cost them to come here tonight to face the world again. A secret club no one else would want to be part of.

Niccolo wondered, despite the entourage of security and advisors around her, if she'd felt as lonely as he had when her family name had been dragged through the mud. She might not have been directly involved in her father's scandalous downfall but he was sure she'd felt the shame and the pressure to clear her name just the same. Had she had support from family or friends, or, like him, had she dealt with it all on her own? There was something about the way she carried herself that made him think the latter. That she portrayed an air of strength to protect that inner fragility he was sure he could see beyond the carefully styled royal. A similar outfit to the one he was wearing tonight, playing the Hollywood superstar to the crowd, kissing a princess without permission, while secretly terrified this could all come to an end again.

If only they had some space away from the cameras and the watching crowd they might be able to confide in each other, compare their troubled lives, perhaps even find solace in one another.

He realised he was still holding her hand and decided he'd clearly been without company too long when he was imagining forging a relationship with the future Queen based on this brief interaction. Realising herself that the introduction had gone beyond the normal polite greeting, Princess Gaia pulled her hand away.

She stepped closer, looking as though she had something to say. Niccolo leaned in so she could speak directly into his ear.

'I guess it's time for us to put on our game

faces, Mr Pernici.' She nodded an acknowledgement before moving on but the eye contact between them lingered a little longer than perhaps
it should have.

There had been something in that recognition
of one another making it impossible for Niccolo
to take his eyes off her. His reward came a few
moments later when she turned back to catch
his eye once more. He smiled and placed his
hand on his heart, afraid he'd lost it so quickly
and easily to someone so out of reach.

Niccolo had known it would be too much. Watching his portrayal of a man on the verge of a breakdown was too close to home for him to remain
in his seat. The last thing he needed was to burst
into tears at his own movie.

'Ana, I think I'm going to duck out for a while,'
he whispered to the one person who'd truly stuck
by him through the worst time of his life.

'But Niccolo, this is your night, your mas-
terpiece.' Her voice gradually got higher as she
extolled all the reasons he should keep his butt
in his chair.

'I've seen it. Overrated if you ask me.' He
dropped a kiss on her head and did his best to
leave with the minimum disruption.

Head bowed and knees bent, he crept past the
other viewers, and took one last glance at the

Princess sitting in the front row. She seemed so engaged in watching him fall apart he should've been proud of his work. Instead, his stomach and his pride plummeted into his expensive leather dress shoes that she should be witness to his actual mental decline.

'Excuse me.' He pushed past the bemused security behemoth at the door, almost gasping for air. To him, the auditorium had become a freak show with the VIP guests invited to ooh and ahh at the downfall of a once-loved actor now reduced to humiliating himself for a pittance. He'd done all that was expected of him so hopefully he could go home as soon as the movie itself had ended.

It was ironic that the budget production, only in existence because no one would touch him, could now herald the resurgence of his career. He couldn't help but think it had come at too high a price.

This was different from the romantic comedies he was famed for, or the few action flicks he'd been lucky to play a part in. For someone infamous for not displaying emotion in his real life, it was all up there on the big screen for the world to see. He wasn't suffering a terminal illness or contemplating his imminent death like his character, but he knew he'd been channelling those overwhelming feelings of his own grief and helplessness to make his character believable. That was why it was a difficult watch for him. It wasn't fiction; it wasn't a performance. It was a man grieving for the life he'd lost through no fault of his own, hiding in plain sight.

He wondered if Princess Gaia could relate to the pain and that powerlessness of the world continuing to spin even though one's life had come to a standstill. If she saw past the story and the character and instead was watching the real Niccolo Pernici reveal a side to him he'd never shown anyone before. That thought was more disturbing than the worry his fans would be turned off by his change of direction.

It wasn't often that Gaia was starstruck. Getting doe-eyed over a film star was not becoming for a princess, or so her mother had reminded her with a sharp elbow to the ribs back at the greeting line.

Given her current circumstances, she never thought she would as much as look at another man. They'd caused enough turmoil in her life to date. There was something about Niccolo Pernici in that short encounter that she'd found...intriguing. A connection between them that she'd been unable to put from her mind. Perhaps it was because they'd both been in the headlines recently for all the wrong reasons, but she'd felt a kinship, a familiarity in him, though they'd never met before. And an attraction she definitely could not afford to indulge in.

To date her relationships had been 'arranged'. Men from the 'right' families, 'good stock', appropriate matches for the daughter of the future King. That hadn't turned out so well when she had a type, leaning towards privileged narcissists as her mother had.

Now she was the future Queen she suspected her choices would be even more limited. In her current position she might not get a choice at all. It was part of the reason she hadn't shared her not so happy news yet. Once the establishment heard she was pregnant they would want her married off to the next available socially acceptable suitor, and she didn't think she had the option to object. An illegitimate child in line to the throne would be unheard of, even in a progressive country which, so far, seemed open to the idea of a future female monarch.

Although she'd done her best to stay away from the press, she knew there had been debates on TV and radio about changing the rules for her. As always, there were those in favour and some against the idea. Either way, she was in the spotlight and under pressure to be a good role model until she got the chance to experience the power and status of her ascension to the throne. Not that she was expecting an easy ride then either. She would have a lot of prejudice to fight, both inside and outside the palace, from traditionalists who wanted to maintain the status quo no matter what.

The only glimpse of happiness she could see cracking through the gloom was the actual birth of this baby. Someone who wouldn't judge Gaia for her choices or her status. At least not until he or she was a teenager, when all bets were off. By the time her bundle of joy was born she expected to have sorted things out with her family and at least have some peace of mind on that front. Until then she had to keep her worries and secrets to herself. Something to keep her awake at night and keep her nerves constantly on edge.

That was why, despite Niccolo's phenomenal portrayal of a man on the brink, she was getting antsy sitting here. She didn't need to be further depressed, and if she was honest she wasn't enjoying watching him fall apart before her eyes. Not when she'd just experienced his charisma first-hand.

What she needed was his usual smouldering, smart-ass romantic lead to make her forget her own tragic love life. She did not need to see him broken and wonder if any of it had been an act, or if she was seeing the toll these past two years had taken on him for real.

Their lifestyles and their reasons for being in the headlines were very different, but they'd both suffered at the hands of the press and the rumour mill. That pain etched on his handsome face she'd seen reflected in the mirror every day her family's name was dragged through the mud, their very existence brought into question. It was no wonder he hadn't been able to watch himself.

She'd noticed him slipping out and he hadn't come back yet. It wasn't so easy for her with Security positioned at every exit and her private bodyguard shadowing her every move. Much needed precautions in the days of terrorist attacks and people who simply bore a grudge against the royal family, but it didn't make their presence any less stifling.

Her bladder was no longer working alongside those societal rules that dictated she shouldn't be seen as a mere mortal who needed such basic amenities as a bathroom either.

'Excuse me, Mother. I'll be back in a few minutes.' She ignored the pointed look and made her escape with her entourage practically announcing her bathroom break to the audience as they got ready to move with her.

'I'm sure Raimondo will suffice for now,' she

told them, exasperated by the whole palaver of simply going to the bathroom. Her head of security nodded, telling the rest of the team to back down.

It was a small concession, very much appreciated. Although she still had to wait for a security sweep of the private cubicle before she was allowed a moment of privacy.

A few minutes later, whilst washing her hands at the sink, she heard voices outside the bathroom door.

'So you're, like, the Princess's bodyguard? That's so cool. Do you know Niccolo too?'

She heard Raimondo grunt in response to whom she assumed was some starry-eyed groupie hoping to find a way to reach her movie idol.

When Gaia peered outside, her big, burly security was paying more attention to the blonde twirling her hair around her finger and feeling his biceps than to his charge. This was her chance for a moment of freedom, some time to breathe without the world watching. She eased the door closed behind her, hitched up her dress and hurried down the corridor like a runaway bride having second thoughts about the man waiting for her at the end of the aisle.

In a way she supposed that was what she was, if her future role as a monarch was the groom in this scenario, with the country waiting for the happy ending. After all, what did she know about running a country? She hadn't been prepped for it the way her father had been. This responsibility had just been dropped on her from a great height, a weight so great she could barely breathe and would possibly leave nothing more of her behind than a dark smudge of the person she'd used to be.

She let herself into a side room where chairs were stacked around the walls and old movie posters lay discarded on a threadbare jazzy carpet. Perhaps once an office, it was now little more than a store room, but to her it represented freedom. That strong need to breathe in fresh air sent her hurrying to the window and wresting the wooden frame up until the cool draught from outside breezed across her skin.

'It is rather oppressive back there, isn't it?'

The deep voice coming from somewhere in the room made her yelp. Now she realised how foolish it had been to ditch her security team and run off on her own. She'd left herself vulnerable to whatever weirdo had been hiding in here, and no one knew where she was. A glance around for a makeshift weapon left her clutching a nearby paintbrush.

'Who's there?' she demanded, thrusting her brush dagger forward.

'What are you going to do—paint me to death?' the voice mocked from the shadows.

'My—my security team will be here soon.'

'I hope not. You look as though you need time out and I don't fancy taking on that hulk of a bodyguard you usually have by your side.' Shadow man stepped out from behind a stack of chairs and Gaia was able to lower her weapon.

'Niccolo? What are you doing here?'

'The same as you, I imagine. Escaping.' He lifted a silver hip flask to his lips and took a swig before offering it to her. She shook her head.

Mr Movie Star didn't look quite as composed as he had during the line-up minus his jacket, his sleeves rolled up and his bowtie hanging loosely around his open collar.

'But it's your movie. Everyone is here to see you.'

He glanced at her through narrowed eyes. 'To see me, or to watch me?'

'Isn't it the same thing?'

Niccolo moved across the room to disarm her, setting the paintbrush back on the bench where she'd found it.

'There are some people who have come with genuine interest in the film, curious to see if it lives up to the hype, but…' He took another drink from his flask and she could smell whisky on his breath. 'I'm sure there are many more out there who want to see me fail, to gossip about me, to believe all the things they've read about me.'

'Do you really believe that?' It saddened her to think people could be that cruel, or that Niccolo could think that on one of the biggest nights of his career.

'Don't you?' He had an infuriating way of turning all questions back on to her, as though she was a mind reader, or someone who was going through the same thing and not enjoying the attention.

Gaia thought about the reasons she was here tonight, of how afraid she was that the very subtle changes of her two-month pregnancy might be noticed and of the repercussions of that. Her breasts were tender, her belly a little softer, but nothing too noticeable, she hoped, and her mother hadn't commented. Now Niccolo had caused her to worry people had come to watch her, to witness her possible downfall too, and would see those tiny changes heralding her pregnancy.

She shuddered at the thought. It was a shame she couldn't enjoy a stiff drink along with him.

'Are you cold? I can close the window and fetch my jacket for you.' He rubbed his hands up and down her arms and quickly generated an inner heat. It had been a couple of months since anyone had touched her and she was enjoying the feel of him against her skin.

'Sorry. I'm probably not supposed to do that, much less even talk to you, Princess.' He dropped his hands and took a step back, that damned sense of etiquette which followed her like a faithful hound robbing her of a further moment of comfort.

'It's fine. I think we're both in need of a break from social niceties. If it's any consolation, I never believed any of those rumours in the papers,' she blurted out, keen for Niccolo to know he had a kindred spirit in her.

It was nice to be able to drop her guard for a little while and simply have a chat without having to choose her every word with caution. Niccolo had been to hell and back with the tabloids, so she trusted him not to share the details of their unexpected meeting. It was difficult to make friends in her position, always wary that any confidences shared would somehow make their way to the press. Alas, this was the privileged but lonely life of a princess.

He cocked his head to one side as though he was deciding whether she was being honest or merely polite. Eventually he mumbled a coy, 'Thanks.'

Gaia wondered how much his ordeal had taken

out of him. She was emotionally exhausted by the constant dissection of her family's behaviour and it wasn't even her who'd caused a scandal. Yet. Niccolo had come under personal attack, his integrity and good character not just called into question but completely eviscerated.

Although he had been a tad forward during their introduction, it had been harmless fun and he seemed a nice enough guy, minus the usual ego and swagger of entitlement she'd met in other celebrities. Perhaps that had been knocked out of him by one woman's unsubstantiated claims which had derailed his career. Yet he'd never once spoken out against her, which spoke of his dignity and integrity and incredible patience.

She found herself wondering if a man like Niccolo Pernici would abandon his responsibilities. If he would have walked away from a pregnant partner and left her to deal with the consequences. She wanted to believe otherwise, that there were men out there who could still be counted upon to do the right thing, but she would for ever be wary now of anyone who crossed her path.

'I think this film will remind people what a great actor you are and all of that terrible gossip will fade into memory.' There was always a bigger scandal waiting in the wings. Her father's affair had replaced the columns on Niccolo's alleged misdemeanours. She could only pray she wouldn't be the next target for public ridicule.

'I hope so, but I assume the movie wasn't to your personal taste, Princess, since you left halfway through?' He was teasing her, his deep brown, almost black, eyes daring her to tell the truth.

'You were amazing but I, uh…let's just say things are a little tough for me right now and I wasn't in the right frame of mind to appreciate it.' She had no desire to offend him no matter how unintentionally when he'd surely had enough criticism for one lifetime.

'You mean you didn't want to be depressed any more than you already are? Kind of why I walked out too. Let's hope the whole audience doesn't feel the same way.'

That made her laugh. Something she thought she'd never do again after all the recent heartache.

'Sorry.' She didn't know how to explain her reaction, her discomfort at seeing him emotionally vulnerable when she hardly knew him. An apology was all she could offer.

'It's fine. I realise you've had a tough time lately too.' His warm smile immediately lessened her guilt and increased another emotion.

An attraction to someone who seemed at ease wearing his heart on his sleeve, encouraging her to do the same and simply be herself. Something which she really didn't need further complicating her life.

'You could say that.' Though he didn't know the half of what she was going through. No one did.

'Sorry I couldn't give you an upbeat, feel-good, forget-about-the-real-world-for-a-while romcom. I guess I just wasn't in the mood at the time.' He ran his finger through his slicked-back hair, dislodging a few errant curls refusing to be tamed.

'I'm not surprised. I don't know how you even managed to get out of bed, much less make your own movie. Didn't you want to just hide away from the world when all of that was going on in the press?' That had been her reaction to finding out about her father, pulling the covers over her head and refusing to face the world until her mother had intervened. She'd been shamed then by her broken-hearted parent, who'd been directly affected by the scandal and still managed to function, outwardly at least. Whatever inner turmoil her mother had been going through she'd kept it to herself, as always. If there was one thing she had learned from her family it was not to give away what was going on behind the royal façade. That was fine when out in public, but it would have been nice to have someone at home who encouraged her to express her feelings, to have someone to talk to and confide in. She hadn't had that sort of relationship with anyone, including her mother. Emotions were something to be contained. Yet no one had taught her how to work past them, through them, or live with them.

She and Niccolo were both trapped, playing roles they didn't want to be in, longing for normal lives away from the public eye. Unfortunately for her that was never going to be a possibility.

'What would that have solved? I still have to make a living. It's not as though you can wake up in the morning and just decide not to be a princess either. This is simply part of who we are and we have to live with it.'

'You could just walk away. Plenty of actors have shunned the spotlight and disappeared into obscurity. It's not so easy for me.' Unless she caused a scandal like her father, except she was the last in the immediate family line and therefore much more likely to cause irreparable damage to the monarchy if she abdicated her position.

'I could, but I love acting so much, and this film has opened up avenues in directing I'm keen to explore too. Until last year it probably was more about the pay check for me but some time in the wilderness has given me perspective on certain things. As pompous as it sounds, I want to leave a legacy behind. I want to be able to tell stories, inform and entertain people at the same time. I'd be happier doing that than sitting counting my fortune somewhere. Don't get me wrong, money helps, but it's not everything.' Niccolo's laugh was as warm as his smile and just as intoxicating. He seemed so far from the wisecracking characters he often played Gaia could see how great an actor he truly was.

'I did enjoy the film you did about the dance instructor, "One More Tango in Rome".' As well as being romantic and sweet, the dancing in that film had been passionate and downright obscene in places. She'd watched one particular scene on repeat. Not that she could admit that to the man standing in front of her, lest she spontaneously combust through embarrassment.

'Ah, yes, a fan favourite.' He did a quick solo waltz around the floor, causing Gaia to burst into applause.

'Did you do the dancing yourself? I mean, did you learn the moves specially for the film?' Her cheeks became suffused with heat at the memory of the tango sequence which led his character and his partner to the bedroom for some more spectacular moves between the sheets.

'We had a really good teacher on set but I think the chemistry with my co-star helped. Do you dance?'

'Only as a social requirement. The Argentine Tango is not on the approved list for princesses. Besides, I'm not sure I could do it justice. The steps seem so complicated I'd be afraid of kicking my partner somewhere inappropriate.'

'It's easy once you know the basics. Here, let me show you.' He held his hand out and Gaia took it willingly.

'Sorry, is this allowed?' he asked, after pulling her into hold.

'Not usually, but at present I'm not in my princess guise, I'm just Gaia.' They'd both forgotten themselves and how they were supposed to behave around one another, but it was nice not to have someone treating her as untouchable, and at the same time feeling almost normal for once.

'I'm not a very good student.' She made her excuses in case she made a fool of herself in front of someone who clearly had talent in this department.

'I'm afraid it's a very close dance.' He'd pulled her so tightly against him she could smell the mix of spicy cologne and man sweat clinging to his skin.

Afraid any attempt to speak would come out as a squeak, she nodded her consent and placed one hand on his shoulder, the other interlaced with his.

'It's about fire and passion. A love-hate, push and pull between partners.' He showed her a few steps, leaving her dizzy as he twirled her around with ease.

'I'm not sure I'm wearing the right outfit for this,' she noted, her body restricted as she attempted to recreate his kicks and flicks.

'Mmm, I think you're right.' He knelt down at her feet and lifted the hem of her dress. 'May I?'

Despite being unsure what he was asking of her, she would have agreed to anything in that moment she was so enraptured with this live re-enactment of his most famous dance.

The rip of fabric sounded through the room as Niccolo deftly made two thigh-high splits in her gown. She gasped as much with delight as shock at the bold move, which wouldn't have been out of place in her once favourite erotic scene. Replaced for ever by this one.

'That's better,' he said, standing up, his eyes and voice both darker than before.

Gaia's mouth went dry as he held her gaze,

lifting her leg to anchor his thigh while they spun around. She could feel the hardness of his body pressed against her softness and her heart was racing from more than the physical exertion. It was exhilarating being in Niccolo's arms doing something illicit and just for her.

Suddenly he threw her effortlessly up into the air and she braced her hands on his shoulders as he slowly lowered her back down his body. She was lost in his eyes, in the sensation of sliding along his torso so intimately, and to what it was doing to her inside.

He twirled her around again and dipped her head back, following the arc of her body with his so their lips were almost touching, their breath mingling in the millimetres between.

Then a camera flashed and the moment was captured. Ruined for ever.

CHAPTER TWO

'OH, HOLY HOTNESS!' As Gaia bit into a slice of wholemeal toast she glanced at the bundle of newspapers stacked neatly on the table and, in her hurry to grab them, accidentally bumped the table with her knee.

She immediately jumped to her feet, watching helplessly as her glass of orange juice sluiced over her silk floral pyjamas and the sharp, irrefutable sight of her and Niccolo on the front page.

If she hadn't been so acutely aware of the implications of said money shot, she would've been impressed by how good they looked together. She took more care to clean the juice off the newspaper than her pyjamas, shaking the excess off onto the marble tiles so she could get another look.

Everyone was going to lose their mind over this picture. She and Niccolo knew there was nothing in it—it hadn't been anything more than an impromptu dance lesson. Okay, so he'd got her a little hot under the halter-neck with his moves, but neither of them had acted upon it.

'What is the meaning of this, Gaia?'

She'd known it would only be a matter of time before her grandfather saw the same head-lines declaring the greatest love affair of the century, false though they were, but he'd been exceptionally quick to find her out here on the terrace. Unfortunately it spoke volumes of his displeasure and urgency to discuss the matter.

'Good morning, Grandfather, Mother.' Although it was her grandfather who was addressing her directly, her mother was hovering in the background. Both had the same disapproving glare trained on her. Just what she needed first thing in the morning with her spoiled breakfast and tabloid scandal.

'How can you sit there, Granddaughter, as though you haven't a care in the world when you've brought our family name into disrepute yet again?' He slammed his hand down on top of the other newspapers, the same photograph displayed on all of the front pages.

'Because I haven't done anything, Grandfather.' Gaia kept her tone measured and calm even though she wanted to scream about the injustice of the pressure on her and dramatically tip over her breakfast table.

'You can see how it looks, Gaia.' Her mother stepped forward to play devil's advocate.

When Gaia and Niccolo had been caught in their compromising position, her mother had been part of the audience. They hadn't known a search had begun during their absence, caught up in their few minutes of liberation from their stifling existence. As soon as the cameras flashed Niccolo had let go of her and her mother had assumed physical control, rushing her back to their waiting limousine and whisking her away from the furore.

'Niccolo was simply showing me a few dance steps, nothing more.' Except in her head. If she'd been thinking logically she would have realised it was inappropriate, but she'd been too caught up in the moment dancing with the handsome movie star to think about how it would look.

'It doesn't look like nothing.' Her grandfather lifted another of the newspapers and shoved it in her face so she was confronted by the image of her and Niccolo, bodies entwined, heads so close it looked as though they were about to kiss.

'We didn't do anything.' Her protest was weaker this time because she knew with the evidence provided no one was ever going to believe her.

'The damage is done. The whole world thinks you and Niccolo Pernici are in a relationship. It's what we do about it now that is important.' Her mother's voice of reason did little to control Gaia's racing pulse. She knew what this meant. It was another scandal, more discussions about the behaviour of the royal family as if they were needed when all they seemed to do was bring negative attention. In a different time they might have had the whole country lining up at the palace gates calling for her head. All of which seemed so unfair when she hadn't actually done anything. She tried not to think about what might happen when her pregnancy came to light.

'Why do we have to do anything? People have misunderstood what happened. Why should I have to explain anything when it's liable to simply make me look guilty of something untoward?' Even if they had been enjoying a secret tryst, caught in the midst of a passionate embrace, it should have been nobody's business. They were two single adults. Regardless that everyone seemed to believe they owned a piece of them because of their very public status.

'You disappeared, Gaia, causing a security alert. This…this is how we found you, together.' Her mother's usual composure began to slip, her voice shrill and full of accusation as she took her turn to point at the incriminating photograph.

'I've said I'm sorry. It wasn't planned. I just needed a break and I ran into Niccolo. We got talking…' And flirting, and dancing, but her mother didn't need to hear that.

It was a shame they had been discovered and been made to feel ashamed for having some time out. The memory of that interlude, a few minutes getting to relax and be herself, was something she would cherish. Goodness knew when she would get to have anything like it again.

Niccolo had been understanding of her situation because he'd been through something similar. He saw her need to escape everything and had provided that with his time and patience, showing her a few dance steps. It hadn't hurt that he was sexy and fun to be around, enough to take her mind off her troubles for a while.

'If you were just talking, the whole world wouldn't think you and this Niccolo were a couple. This isn't just intimate, it's damn near pornographic. After your father's behaviour this is going to look as though you share the same moral code. We cannot afford to lose any more respect, Gaia. I thought I could trust you.'

Her old-fashioned grandfather might be over-reacting to what was essentially an innocent dance but she could see his point. People were going to assume they were together and with a baby on the way it would be easy to believe Niccolo was the father. In seven months' time this wasn't going to be something she could simply brush off. It needed to be addressed now or there would be implications for both of them further down the line.

The die had been cast, even though it was false. Any denial that they were together would make a liar out of her when the baby was born, with Niccolo seen as an absentee father through absolutely no fault of his own. Her family was right—this was a crisis, bigger than they knew.

'I'll speak to Niccolo. I'm sorry to have caused you both further pain. I'll fix this.' She didn't know how, only that she had to. The future of the family and the country depended on it. Poor Niccolo had no idea what he'd got himself involved in.

'The whiff of a royal romance on top of your critical success means you're in more demand than ever. I've been fielding calls from journalists and movie execs since your escapades with our beloved princess last night.' Ana had been thrilled with the publicity this morning, calling Niccolo at seven a.m.

'It was only a dance.' He hadn't shared her

enthusiasm upon seeing the photograph on the front page of every newspaper. Not only had it pulled focus away from his film and onto a non-existent relationship, but it had also captured the very second he'd thought about kissing Gaia.

Looking at himself, lost in the moment, was almost as exposing as seeing himself on the big screen. His raw, naked want for the woman whose soft curves had been tight against him was there on display. There was even something in the way she was looking at him, as though he only had to say the word and she was his, that made the evidence against them even more damning. It was no wonder everyone had lost their minds when it was so clearly more than a dance. Yet their intention had only been to find a little peace away from the crowd.

Neither of them had left that room intending to create a stir; quite the opposite. They'd been oblivious to the commotion surrounding her disappearance until the flash of a camera alerted them to the fact they had an audience for their private dance. Gaia had been whisked away with no chance to say goodbye or anything else. He wished they'd been left alone to enjoy some quiet time and each other's company. Instead now everyone was invested in a relationship that could never be. Even if there had been a spark between them last night, the interest generated would ensure nothing further would happen with the eyes of the world upon them. Given time he knew the publicity would fade away but he regretted letting his guard down and causing them both this extra hassle.

'Well, I think you're going to have to release some sort of statement because my phone is in meltdown with everyone trying to get the scoop. Anyway, I'm calling to say good job on the film and the extra publicity, intentional or not. Let me know what you want to do about addressing these rumours and I'll clear my schedule. You're my number one, Niccolo.' She hung up and, though he appreciated Ana's support, Niccolo knew he was only her number one for today. Ana had been loyal to him during his struggles but she was still a businesswoman and he knew she'd prioritised other clients during that time, just as she would when the public lost interest in this non-event. That was why she wanted him to act now and capitalise on the publicity it had generated to keep the momentum going around the film hype. Except he knew how much it would cost Gaia to draw further interest.

Last night had only happened because she'd been seeking an escape from the attention. Even hinting that there was something going on between them would encourage more of the harassment she had no doubt encountered during the reporting on her father's antics. He would never knowingly invite the sort of pain and suffering he'd gone through these past years into anyone's life and especially not the life of someone like Gaia, who had done nothing to deserve it. On both occasions she'd been an unwitting participant in a scandal, unfortunately caught in the crossfire of public appetite for salacious gossip and men around her who couldn't control themselves.

He blamed himself for this incident, led so quickly into temptation by her vulnerability and beauty. A better man would have taken her back to safety and known his place. Not Niccolo Pernici. He'd allowed himself a flirtation, a physical connection, and an almost kiss, without considering the consequences now facing his partner. Gaia would be judged now worse than ever.

She was the future Queen, with the entire monarchy resting on her shoulders, and he'd jeopardised that for one moment of self-indulgence. He'd wanted her and now the world knew that, could see it for themselves, and had concocted a story around it. It was going to be up to him to give a plausible explanation without destroying either of their reputations. He had no desire to put himself, nor Gaia, through the hell he'd experienced because of the last falsehood he'd been accused of. Even if there was the ring of truth around this one because last night had been about more than a dance lesson. It had been a meeting of minds, two lost souls connecting and finding comfort in one another, along with that flare of passion he was sure came from more than the steps he'd shown her.

Now he had to find a way of putting everything right or risk the wrath of the house of Benetti.

Niccolo's palms had been sweating more at the prospect of facing Gaia and her family at the palace than at his premiere, despite the air-conditioned luxury car which had driven him here.

The very officious call requesting his attendance was not completely unexpected but a nerve-racking experience none the less. He supposed he was a very big part of their current problem so it made sense he should be part of the solution too. Hopefully they could work together to clear up this simple misunderstanding and then they'd probably never cross paths again.

Niccolo experienced a sudden pang, an emptiness opening up in his chest at the very thought.

It had been some time since he'd been that close to anyone, physically or otherwise, and if Gaia had been anyone else he might have explored the connection they seemed to have. As it was, he'd be lucky if he was allowed to even be in the same room as her again.

Neither of them had thought that her brief disappearance would cause a full lockdown of the auditorium, with a search team combing all areas, on high alert for a possible breach of security and threat to her life. Needless to say there had been more than a photographer witnessing their passionate clinch and he could still hear her mother's horrified gasp at their discovery. The family and their advisors were going to haul him over the coals even though they hadn't actually done anything other than play hooky from their responsibilities for a little while. Although in their short time together there had definitely been sparks flying, and given the chance they could very well have burned the whole building down with the passion flaring between them. The reality of their very different lives had soon poured cold water over that notion.

So they weren't in a relationship, or even involved in a salacious fling, but there had been something between them. He'd felt it, from the moment he'd dared to lay his hands on the princess in the greeting line. If he was honest he'd thought about what it would be like to be more intimate with her. He'd taken the opportunity in that store room to get closer. Perhaps that moment during their dance, that instant desire had arisen from their understanding of one another's circumstances, that recognition of a troubled soul in need of company and comfort. Gaia was beautiful, there was no doubt, but she also possessed a fragility, an innocence that called to his inner Neanderthal. It wasn't that he wanted to club her over the head and carry her off to his cave, but he had wanted to make her his during that dance, become her protector so no one could hurt her.

Great job he'd done of that. Now not only was she dealing with her family's troubles but also the world's press was screaming about their alleged relationship. It would almost have been easier if it were true. At least then they could have confirmed it and moved on. Here, they were trapped by the truth.

After stripping off his jacket and shoes to go through body scanners, and an intimidating security team who took way too much interest in his person, he was escorted through the halls of the palace at breakneck speed.

'Where exactly am I going? What am I doing here?' he asked, whizzing past oversized oil

portraits and elaborate gold-embellished tap-
estries on the walls.

He'd assumed it was for a crisis meeting to
discuss what steps were to be taken to minimise
the damage done to the Princess's reputation.
The brief call from Gaia's secretary hadn't given
much away, simply asking him to attend at the
family's request. For all he knew he was on his
way to the tower now, to be held there for ever
as an example of what could happen to com-
moners who dared sully the Princess's virtue.

The well-dressed member of staff halted his
whirlwind tour through the palace long enough
to look at Niccolo, his long nose tilted high into
the air. 'The Princess has asked to see you in
her private rooms. I think you know why.'

He was off again, apparently keen to dis-
charge his responsibility of the latest man to
embarrass the royal family. He was sure he
would meet with a lot more disdain before the
day was over. However, he was relieved that it
was Gaia he was coming to see and not facing
the entire royal family in its might. She would
be upset and regretful but that might be easier
to deal with than the King blasting him for his
inappropriate behaviour.

'Mr Niccolo Pernici to see you, Your Royal
Highness.' Mr Uppity opened a door and announced him to the room with a bow.

'Thank you, Vitale. That will be all for now.'
Gaia sounded much more guarded than she had
the last time they'd met, each word crisp and
thought out.

Niccolo couldn't be certain if this was a direct result of this morning's revelations or if
she usually talked like this and their conversations were the exception, where she'd spoken
freely. Only time and a further audience with
her would tell, but he hoped she knew she could
still talk to him.

The reverential Vitale bowed and took his
leave, closing the doors behind him and leaving Niccolo alone with Gaia.

'I hope there's no one out looking for you
again. I'm not sure anyone would believe us a
second time that this was all totally innocent.'

Gaia gave a smile but it did not reach her
eyes. 'Please, sit.'

She stood and directed him towards a throne-
shaped armchair upholstered in a sage-green
fabric, the arms moulded into golden scrolls.
In a modern apartment it would have looked
tacky but here it fitted right in. The whole scene
looked like something out of a Renaissance
painting and he couldn't quite believe he was
in the middle of it.

The heavily gilded room, cluttered with large
free-standing vases and silk screens, should

have drawn the eye, but Niccolo couldn't look away from Gaia. She was wearing an emerald-green trouser suit with a white silk blouse, looking as beautiful and elegant as ever, and, though he'd dressed formally for the occasion in a tailored navy suit, he still felt underdressed in her presence.

'I hope you've been as thorough checking for photographers as your security have in searching me,' he joked again, attempting to hide his nerves. Being here in the palace made things even more awkward between them when he was reminded of Gaia's status and how out of place he was.

Another forced smile as she carefully took a seat, perching on the edge of the love seat—embellished with painted images of flora and fauna—opposite. 'Security is at an all-time high. Grandfather demanded it.'

He could only imagine the heated conversations with her family which must have gone on here this morning. It wasn't fair, especially on Gaia, that they couldn't enjoy one moment of fun without its becoming a national incident.

'I'm sorry I've got you into such a mess. Should I write my last will and testament now or will it give me something to do when I'm imprisoned in the tower for the next hundred years?'

'You mean you didn't get your affairs into order before coming here?' Gaia gasped, then lapsed into a genuine smile he wished he could keep there for ever.

'So how much trouble are we in?'

She screwed up her face, her nose crinkling like that of a cute bunny snuffling in the grass. 'Huge.'

'Ugh, I was afraid of that.' He slumped back into the chair. Though his playful demeanour had managed to thaw Gaia's initial cold front towards him, it couldn't hide the pain their unexpected dalliance had obviously caused her.

'Grandfather thinks people will believe this is proof I sleep around too. Just like my father.' Her bottom lip wobbled as she spoke, and he would have hugged her if he could be sure it wasn't going to cause her more problems.

'That's ridiculous. It's one photograph, and we're not even doing anything in it.' It would be different if they had been caught in an actual clinch, but it was only a dance.

Gaia dabbed a handkerchief to her eyes before giving permission to any tears to actually fall. 'It doesn't matter, it's what the picture implies. You know people will have drawn their own conclusions.'

Unfortunately he did, and once that happened it was near impossible to change their minds.

'So what if we were an item, what would it matter? You have the right to have a life, the same as I do.' Okay, so it wasn't true, but if they let readers and journalists make their minds up the way he'd done these past two years, how much harm could it cause? It wasn't as though they were being accused of anything untoward, simply of being in a relationship. If they let things play out and naturally fade away from the public interest they could probably weather this.

However, his opinion did little to erase the worry etched on her brow.

'I don't. Every move I make, every decision, is scrutinised, Niccolo. My behaviour reflects on the whole family, just as my father's did. No offence, but you're an actor, not of noble birth. I really shouldn't have been fraternising with you and certainly not alone.' It pained her to say that—he could see it in the red tinge of her cheeks and the way she was almost strangling the handkerchief in her hands—but he wasn't offended by her honesty, he appreciated it.

'You were slumming it, in other words.' The idea amused him, teasing her, even more so, to try and keep things light and all the bad stuff at bay.

'That's not… I didn't mean…' She caught his smirk, grabbed an ivory silk cushion from behind her and chucked it at him. 'You're insufferable.'

'Are we breaking up already? You could re-lease that as your statement—"Niccolo and I are no longer together as I find him altogether insufferable".'

'This is serious, Niccolo. It could jeopardise my position in the family, and without that…'

She didn't need to say the rest when they both knew she'd end up as an outcast like her father, who hadn't been seen or heard from since his departure. It was hard to garner sympathy for a man who'd cheated on his wife and caused his own downfall, but Gaia was different—she was innocent.

'Okay, okay, so why can't we just say what happened? We ran into each other and you expressed an interest in dancing. I showed you a few moves and that's when the photographers arrived.' It was clear they had to address the rumours somehow in an effort to protect Gaia when he should never have laid hands on her in the first place.

She gave a heavy sigh, her lips pursed with blatant annoyance. 'Because no one is going to believe the truth. We will both look like liars.'

The weight of her words settled heavily on

his chest as he realised it wasn't just Gaia's reputation and position at risk here. It had taken him two years to fight his way back from the last scandal to befall him. He wondered what it was about him that made people ready to believe the worst of him. Was it his profession, his alleged wealth, or did he simply have an untrustworthy face? Whatever it was, Gaia was right—as far as onlookers believed, they were an item, and to deny it, to walk away, would look cold and callous. He'd probably stand accused of taking advantage of her at a vulnerable time and dumping her when he'd had his fun. If they went down this path he stood to risk everything again.

He'd poured his heart and soul into making that film, which had managed to get him his life back. It wasn't something he'd be in a hurry to lose a second time and he doubted making another successful solo film would be easy to do. Next time he mightn't be able to claw his way out of the darkness, a place he never wanted to be again. Alone, afraid of what his future held, and unable to share his feelings with anyone. It was fear which kept him captive, the worry that if he showed his emotions he might not recover from it. That he might end up like that grieving child who'd barely made it through the loss of his mother.

He'd been lucky his film had been a success but in the future he might not be as strong, a recovery impossible. As Gaia had said, this was serious.

'We could fake a relationship, go along with the idea that we're a couple for a few months, make a few public appearances together, then split when interest inevitably dies down. It will be an amicable, mutual separation, ensuring there's no story for the press to follow up on.' He was animated, bouncing in his seat with enthusiasm for the plan which had suddenly sprung to mind. It wouldn't cost either of them anything to go with the flow for the time being and it wouldn't be any hardship to spend time with Gaia. If anything it meant he could get to know her a little better without worrying about the usual hurdles in a relationship. Yes, faking it was the way to go.

'That's not going to work.'

'I know it's not ideal, nothing about this situation is. But everyone already thinks we're together. Where's the harm in a little white lie now to save both of our skins?' Was the idea of even pretending to be with him so repellent? Maybe she hadn't been completely convinced of his innocence in the rumours his ex had created. It was not only a blow to his more fragile than usual ego, but also a personal slight when he thought they'd made a genuine connection. Despite all the trouble, he'd got the impression Gaia might even like him. After two years of emotional turmoil his radar for such things must be totally malfunctioning.

When Gaia didn't respond, he knew he'd got things completely wrong and tried to backtrack.

'It was just an idea. I know lying is the very thing you want to avoid doing, but—'

'It's not that.' Her eyes darted around the room as though she was expecting a photographer to jump out from behind the curtains or the fireplace.

'Well, what is it, Gaia? Whatever it is we're both in this together and I promise not a word of this conversation will leave this room. Maybe we don't say anything and just avoid each other? After all, our paths hadn't ever crossed until last night.' It would be a shame if he didn't get to see or speak to her again when she'd been the first person he'd met who could relate to his lifestyle and the impact negative press could have on a person.

'That's not going to work either.'

He was racking his brains for a solution along with the possible reason why she was convinced they were set to fail.

'We could always go out on a date. At least

that way we wouldn't be lying and we might actually—'

'I'm pregnant,' she cried, leaving them both in a state of shock.

CHAPTER THREE

'I KNOW IT was a sexy dance but I'm pretty sure you can't get pregnant that way. I would've thought your private royal tutors would've taught you about the birds and the bees by now.' Apparently humour was Niccolo's go-to response to her life-changing news.

'Niccolo, don't you see? There will be consequences for both of us when this gets out.' Sitting ever so still now, she appeared more delicate than the china figures posing on the mantelpiece above the fire.

Despite his feeble attempt to lighten the mood, the gravity of the situation was becoming increasingly apparent. Gaia was next in line to the throne, unmarried, and pregnant. With the incriminating photograph of them in a compromising position plastered over the papers and the television it would be impossible to persuade anyone he wasn't the father to her unborn child.

'Yes. I'm sorry. Forgive me. You must be under

tremendous strain. I hope your family are supporting you.' He was trying to console her, understanding why this was such a big deal and why none of his solutions were feasible. No matter if they denied, faked or began a relationship, people would put two and two together and come up with a baby daddy. Unless the real father was on the scene and ready to accept responsibility. Judging by the now sobbing Princess, he doubted that was the case.

'I haven't told them yet.'

Another hurdle for her to overcome and she really needed someone in her corner. He knelt down at her side and took her hand.

'I'm sure it will be all right. It will come as a shock but in this day and age it doesn't have the same stigma to have a baby outside of wedlock.'

'This is the royal family we're talking about.' Her liquid-gold eyes implored him to understand her situation.

'I know you're not married but there's still time for the father to step up.' So far there had been no mention of the man she had been in a relationship with. Surely he was the one who should be by her side supporting her and taking the flak from her family for ruining her reputation. Although she shouldn't have to feel shame, as though sex and pregnancy were new concepts. Especially to the royal family.

It was a bombshell now but he was sure everyone would get over it eventually. In his case, two years had been sufficient time to suffer before the world moved on and he was supposed to forget it ever happened.

'People are going to think it's your baby, Niccolo.'

He looked at her, words refusing to form in his head or on his lips, his brain working overtime to process what she was saying.

'But it's not.' It was the only argument he could come up with, and one which wouldn't easily win him a place on the debating team.

'I know that, and you know that, but that's how it's going to look.' Her smooth forehead was now worried with frown lines.

'And how will the actual father feel about that? Won't he be keen to set the record straight?' If Gaia was his partner, pregnant with his baby, he wouldn't want anyone else claiming paternity. Nor would he stand back and let speculation run rife, causing immeasurable suffering to her and her family, without saying anything.

'He doesn't want to be involved, with me or the baby. I realised too late he didn't want anything serious.'

'You don't get more serious than being a father. It's not something which should be taken lightly, and if he was that concerned perhaps he should've taken precautions to stop it happening.' He may have been crossing the line but it was a touchy subject for him when his own father hadn't been keen on taking responsibility for his child either. When Niccolo's mother had died his father had acted like a born-again bachelor, whose traumatised child had been more of an inconvenience than someone who needed his love and comfort. Not so much these days, when his offspring's celebrity status was something he exploited for the benefit of his love life as well as his business dealings.

That was why Niccolo preferred to keep things light and casual in his personal life, trying to avoid complicated entanglements, because he didn't want to get to the point where a rejection would cause him further irreparable emotional damage. Unfortunately Christina had failed to accept his boundaries and caused more drama than he'd ever anticipated.

'A mother doesn't get a choice. At least, not one I'm willing to consider.' There was a steeliness to her words that already made her a natural mother and he admired her strength in the face of such an uncertain future. She might accept the situation but it was going to be difficult for her family and the nation.

'I'm sure you'll be a great mother and when the baby gets here everything else will be forgotten. Everyone will see how strong and capable you are. A more than suitable leader for this modern country.' He believed everything he said because she came across as such a genuine, down-to-earth person who cared about doing the right thing. Gaia would be an amazing mum, raising a child and simultaneously running a country, defying convention and proving her place in society. He could tell by the way she cared so deeply about people, especially the little one growing inside her. Not everyone might have been so resolute in the circumstances.

'This affects you too, Niccolo. The press think we're together. How is it going to look if we go our separate ways and I have a baby a few months down the line?'

He listened to everything she was saying, saw the picture of them so clearly in his mind it would be natural to believe there'd been a pregnancy as a result. It was easy to imagine the follow-up news article, once again painting him as a villain: *Movie Star Leaves Princess Heartbroken and Pregnant.*

The truth didn't matter when the headline would sell millions worldwide. So much for his comeback. More bad press, especially if it involved hurting the country's beloved princess, would finish his career for good this time.

The gut punch knocked him onto his backside, his legs outstretched on a priceless antique rug. He dropped his head into his hands. Apparently he didn't have to do anything for people to believe the worst of him. Despite his attempts to avoid emotional entanglements, he couldn't seem to escape them.

'I'm sorry, but how did this become my problem? We were only together for a few minutes and, though that's all it takes in some instances, we both know nothing happened. I like you, Gaia, but I'm not prepared to stand back and watch my life fall apart again over another false rumour. You need to put this straight. I know the father doesn't want to be involved but neither do I. That might sound heartless, but being a parent was never in my plans, even in error.' Niccolo was aware that his voice was getting louder but the injustice of what was happening was too great for him to simply stand back and let it overwhelm him again. He was in danger of letting his emotions get the better of him for once, the royal palace an unusual and untimely place for the events of the past years to finally catch up with him. It wasn't Gaia's fault, it wasn't his or anyone else's fault. His life was simply a catalogue of unfortunate events.

'I'm sorry. I know none of this is your fault, Niccolo. You're right, I'll deal with it. I'll get the car to take you back.' Gaia reached for the phone to call Niccolo's getaway vehicle.

It was too much to ask of him; he hadn't done anything, though she had noted the part where he'd said he liked her. Not enough to stick around and support her apparently, like the other men in her life. A shame when she thought she'd found someone who understood her, who saw through the façade and understood her. She'd thought Niccolo was someone she could talk to but it was apparent he wanted to distance himself as far as possible from this mess. Not that she could blame him—she'd do the same if she could.

Niccolo's hand covered hers before she could dial.

'There's no need for that. I'm sorry for overreacting. It's just a lot after everything else lately. There was so much riding on this movie and, well, I guess you know what it's like to be under pressure.' The apology in his gaze would have been enough but the compassion she saw softening his features was enough to make the tears start falling again.

'I just feel so alone, Niccolo.' She couldn't help it; the past months of worry, of keeping this huge secret to herself, finally caught up with her. Her shoulders were heaving as the sobs ripped from her chest. Up until now she

hadn't dared share her predicament with anyone, not ready to see the disappointment staring back at her, or worse, that the information
would be leaked elsewhere. She'd only told Niccolo because he would be affected when the
news did come out and she trusted him not to
tell anyone else in the meantime. It hadn't been
her intention to ruin his life, or to fall apart on
him.

Yet, despite dropping this baby bombshell
in the middle of his life, he was gathering her
into his arms and letting her cry all over him.
It should have been an awkward hug with Niccolo kneeling on the floor trying to comfort
someone he'd only met the night before, but the
strength of his embrace told her it was genuine
concern, not merely a token act. That was sufficient for her to relax into it, revelling in the
warmth and protection of his hard body and the
knowledge that he cared. She couldn't remember the last time she'd experienced any of that.

'I'm not going to leave you to deal with this
on your own. We'll think of some way of getting through this.'

With Niccolo wrapped around her, whisper-
ing words of comfort in her ear, she was inclined to believe him even if she knew it was a
big ask. He understood the gravity of the situation because he was still living through what

was probably one of the worst times of his life caused by gossip and bad publicity. It wasn't fair to get him involved but that ship had sailed with the click of a camera. Selfishly she wanted Niccolo to be in this with her so she had someone in her corner, albeit somewhat reluctantly.

Eventually, he loosened his hold and sat back on his haunches. Though Gaia could still feel the imprint of his embrace on her skin, it was colder without him. She wondered if there was a position available for a royal hugger to take care of her needs when she was feeling low. He'd never be out of work.

'Thanks,' she said, dabbing at her eyes and knowing it was pointless trying to maintain some dignity when she'd probably cried her make-up off in front of him. 'Sorry. I'm sure I look a sight.'

'You're beautiful, as always,' he said with a warm smile before getting to his feet and taking a seat away from her.

They were words she'd heard throughout her life and never put any store in them. After all, it had been her job to look pretty in the background, mauled and manipulated by stylists paid to make her look her best. But hearing them from Niccolo in one of her most vulnerable moments meant a lot to her. She realised, to further her dismay when it would only complicate matters further, that she still wanted him to like her. There was a part of her that needed to know she hadn't imagined that frisson between them last night before the whole world had crashed in around them.

'Thanks,' she said again, her spirits lifted a little thanks to the charming man who'd had the misfortune to get caught in her messy affairs.

'So…naming the deadbeat dad is out of the question?'

''Fraid so. I made a promise, and to be honest, after the way he's behaved, I'd prefer to keep him out of my life.' Believing Stefan loved her had been the greatest mistake of all. He'd let her think he was someone she could rely on in a world where she had no one. Her parents had their own issues they were dealing with, both personally and publicly, and she was something of an afterthought to them. That changed when her grandfather advocated for her to be the next in line to the throne and she became the focus of attention. Although it still didn't make it any easier to confide her fears about the future when one hint she wasn't coping would have sent the whole establishment into a tailspin.

This new development definitely would.

'Okay, I get that. I sometimes think I'd have been better off without my own dad when he so clearly had no interest in raising me after my mother died.'

'Niccolo, I'm so sorry. I had no idea—'

He held his hand up to interrupt her before they got into sharing stories about difficult childhoods. It was probably for the best when it would be difficult for anyone to empathise with her struggles after being born into a life of privilege.

'This isn't about me. I'm just running through our options.'

She liked his use of 'our'—it made her feel as though she wasn't on her own.

'We can rule him out completely. Best forgotten. Hopefully never to be heard from again.'

Her outburst made him grin.

'Message received loud and clear. I'm guessing we can't call it an immaculate conception either, so…what about we make up a partner? He's dead, you're essentially a widow and don't want to be reminded of your heartbreak so you'll not be commenting any further on the matter.' He looked so pleased with himself she hadn't the heart to tell him why she didn't think that would work either, but Niccolo was the one person she thought she didn't have to mollify for appearances' sake.

'Think of the timing though. I'm two months pregnant. If I had a partner I loved enough to have a baby by and lost him, it's still going to look bad that I hooked up with you so soon. That would have the opposite effect from the one I want. I'm not the kind of girl who sleeps around so I'd rather people didn't believe that of me.' It was important to her what others thought, perhaps too much. If she did have a very active sex life that wouldn't have been anybody's business either but, since she didn't, she'd rather not have that kind of reputation. It wasn't one which would command respect from certain quarters when her time as Queen finally came.

Niccolo's head dropped, as though the weight of it all had suddenly become too much, his body weary from trying to project a strength that was now waning. She knew exactly how that felt.

'Okay, so back to the drawing board. You're not going to be able to hide this pregnancy for ever.'

'You're pregnant?' As if the situation couldn't get any worse, a royal entourage including her mother and grandfather had chosen that moment to enter the room and Gaia knew things were never going to be the same again.

Niccolo scrambled to his feet and bowed. 'Your Majesty.'

Though he was in the palace, the arrival of the

King was no less intimidating. The way Gaia was so open with him made him forget who he was actually dealing with, but now he was faced with her family he was reminded what a serious situation he was caught up in.

Gaia too got to her feet, looking so pale and fragile he was afraid she might break. 'Grandfather, this is Niccolo Pernici,' she said, bowing her head in respect.

'I know who he is. I just don't understand how he has the audacity to stand in my home after the very public display he engaged you in last night. And now you're telling us you're pregnant, I assume to this man, unless you're more like your father than we thought?' he boomed, demonstrating why Gaia had been so afraid to tell him the news herself.

'But Grandfather—'

'Gaia, your grandfather has a right to be angry. You know the impact this will have on the country. How could you do this? How could you be so careless and stupid? You know what we've been through.' The tall, graceful brunette Niccolo knew to be Gaia's mother, Princess Amara, moved to her side, not to comfort her but to chastise her further for something she was already beating herself up about.

Niccolo couldn't simply stand back and watch

them maul her as though she had committed the crime of the century.

'Your Majesty.' He nodded to each in turn. 'I know the circumstances are less than ideal and this morning's headlines haven't helped, but I don't think berating Gaia is going to fix things either. She needs our support.'

'Do you comprehend the seriousness of impregnating my granddaughter out of wedlock, Mr Pernici?'

Neither of them had dared contradict the King's misunderstanding of the baby's parentage and Niccolo didn't think telling him there was another man involved would placate him in any way. If anything, it would further enrage him and Gaia didn't deserve any more of a pile-on.

'I understand that this is a very delicate matter—'

'Are you going to step up to your responsibilities and marry my granddaughter?'

'Pardon me?'

'Grandfather, no, Niccolo isn't—'

In that second Niccolo believed there was only one option available to both of them. A single deed which could save both of their reputations and save them from any more of the King's ire. It didn't matter what he did to try and distance himself from the whole scandal, as far as everyone was concerned he was involved.

'Yes, we're getting married,' he announced, surprising himself as much as everyone else in the room. He put an arm around Gaia's shoulders and she leaned into him as if he were the only thing keeping her upright.

The only way he could see to salvage his reputation and his livelihood before they were ground into the dirt again was to act as though he *was* this baby's father. It wasn't a role he'd ever wanted, and he didn't know how he was going to fake his way through it. He would have to embrace the part completely. Having an emotionally distant parent was as damaging as losing one. Gaia's baby didn't deserve to feel as though it was a burden, so he would have to come to terms with accepting complete responsibility for this child and not simply be a token father figure. He had no intention of imitating his dad but it wasn't going to be easy raising someone else's child. Especially in these circumstances, where he'd been forced into a corner if he wanted to keep his career and the life he'd just got back.

There was no way of explaining to a baby that he was merely a stunt dad, one for show to replace the real deal. So he had to accept he was going to be a dad for real, along with his role as a fake husband. He'd always been afraid of having children himself in case he kept that emotional detachment which had caused him so much trouble in his romantic relationships. Putting himself in this position was forcing him to face those long-held issues head-on.

Christina's antics had made him question the type of man he was for her to have treated him the way she had. He must have really hurt her to receive such vitriol from her, and subsequently from the press and general public. His actions in the past had been his attempt to avoid unnecessary pain but apparently that hadn't been the case. It was important to him that he wasn't the same heartless monster as had been portrayed in the papers, or the same one as his father, disregarding the feelings of his grief-stricken son. He wanted to get over that inability to forge a meaningful relationship and perhaps he could do that with a baby. Children needed to be loved, and gave love back unconditionally. He shouldn't have to fear rejection from that relationship at least.

That was if Gaia agreed to this whole charade. After all, she didn't know him or his motives for doing this. It was asking her to trust that he wanted to do the right thing for both of them.

'Niccolo?' She was looking up at him, those big eyes searching his face for answers.

He gave her a squeeze of reassurance that everything was going to be okay. This was for her as much as it was for him, to give her the sense of security neither of them had had for a long time. Though it shouldn't be the way, she needed a father for her baby to keep her family and the rest of the country happy. More than that, Gaia needed a partner who would support her in both her personal and public lives.

'This might just work, Your Majesty.' Another man presented himself in the room from behind the King's intimidating bulk. Tall and waspish, he thrust forward a folder of papers for the King to flick through.

'What is this, Guglielmo?'

'The family's popularity soared with this morning's headlines. It appears the country is interested in a romance between Princess Gaia and this movie star.' He looked down his proud nose as though he was more than a mere royal advisor. No doubt someone else for Gaia to validate her life choices to.

Thank goodness he was only accountable to himself. He expected to give himself a really good talking-to about making spontaneous grand gestures without fully thinking things through. Getting married in this instance didn't seem as big a deal as a marriage based on that flitting ideal of love. This was a means to an end, emotions not included. As long as he made that clear from the outset, and they could raise this child as a platonic couple, they might just ride this out.

CHAPTER FOUR

GAIA GLANCED BETWEEN her fake fiancé and her family. At least her grandfather no longer resembled a bearded tomato. She would never have forgiven herself if she'd caused him to have a heart attack. Her mother too no longer looked as though her only daughter had broken her heart. Even Guglielmo had an uncharacteristic air of optimism about him. It was a shame it was all built on a lie. However, she couldn't bring herself to tell them that. It was much easier to go along with Niccolo's crazy get-out scheme for now.

'How far along are you?'

'A couple of months.' She'd been in denial for most of that time because admitting it meant addressing the matter and she'd been too frightened to do so. It was only with Niccolo's help that she was able to get through this now.

He was probably worried he'd end up in the tower for treason, so he'd concocted this story. Once he was outside the palace gates they wouldn't see him for dust. She'd go along with this version of events until she had a different plan in place, but she knew better than to rely on any man.

'The wedding will have to happen soon. Before you show.' Guglielmo looked her up and down as though he were better than a pregnant princess.

The first thing Gaia was going to do when she came to power was surround herself with more supportive, forward-thinking aides. People she could trust, and who believed in her. Not flunkeys with a superiority complex. He was part of the establishment and therefore part of the problem when it came to the monarchy keeping up with the times. People of his ilk wanted things to stay the same, under their control. They pulled the strings around here and that was why she posed a threat.

She was a modern woman with a mind of her own. For now she was still trapped by the regime because of the respect she had for her grandfather, but when her time came she was going to shake things up. It was no longer enough for her to look pretty and have babies, she wanted to make a difference. Not be a powerless puppet with the patriarchy still making all the decisions for her.

'Announcements have to be made, arrangements for other heads of state to get here…' As Guglielmo worked out the finer details with the family, Gaia watched the colour drain from Niccolo's usual olive complexion.

This was all new to him, a glimpse into the future he was going to have with her if he insisted on seeing this through.

'You don't have to do this, Niccolo. There's still time to back out,' she whispered to him whilst the others were busy making wedding plans on their behalf.

He considered her words for a moment too long before he smiled again. 'I want to do this. For you.'

'But why? What's in this for you?' She wanted to know why she should trust him, what made him different from anyone else. Whether he was someone she should be with even in a fake marriage.

'Must be my shining-knight complex. I see a princess in distress and I ride right in there on my trusty steed to save the day.'

She rolled her eyes at the impression he did of said knight galloping to the rescue.

'Naturally, we're going to have to consult our lawyers on this too and draw up some legal papers including a prenuptial agreement and a non-disclosure agreement. You will understand the need for the family to protect themselves in the event of the marriage breaking down.' Guglielmo addressed Niccolo directly with no hint of embarrassment about suggesting this alliance would fail before it had even begun.

Even though the whole relationship had been concocted on the spot, it still stung that the idea of her future marriage wasn't being taken seriously. That it was a risk, a liability, rather than a celebration.

'I understand.' Niccolo gave his approval, and acceptance of the situation, probably to get rid of the royal posse as soon as possible.

Gaia held her tongue until they had all left the room, although she didn't miss her mother's pointed stare. The one that said they would be having a word in private later. She wasn't looking forward to lying under direct scrutiny, afraid her mother would see through the lies and force a confession from her, rendering this all a wasted effort on Niccolo's part. He was being chivalrous to a fault going along with this, at extensive personal cost. The interference from 'the establishment' so far was nothing compared to what he'd have to put up with once he became a member of the family. If he didn't run away screaming first.

'Seriously, I want to understand your reasons for going into this before I do.'

It occurred to her that she still had a choice

of sorts too. She could say no to this ludicrous idea of a sham marriage and confess she was pregnant by another man who didn't want to be with her. It could leave her in social limbo and possibly cause the fall of the monarchy but it was an option.

'I wouldn't have made the suggestion if I wasn't going to see it through, Gaia. Marriage has never been something I was interested in when I've seen so many end badly. However, this would be more of a business deal, I suppose. Something which suits both of us. It gets your family off your back and the press off mine. Hopefully once the actual ceremony is over we can both get on with our lives. The marriage would be in name only behind closed doors. If that's acceptable to you?'

Gaia could only imagine the millions of hearts breaking as he proposed this deal. Yes, it was a slap to the ego that a man would only consider marrying her because his career depended on it, but it seemed the most palatable idea right now. This way she got to keep her home, her family and her status, which might not be the case if she was honest about her circumstances.

'What about the baby?'

'I'm pledging myself to both of you.'

'So you'll raise it as your own? I want to be

clear from the outset so there's no misunderstanding.'

Niccolo took more time over his answer, which could only be a good thing. It was a big decision to take on someone else's baby and she didn't want him to agree on a whim, only to decide fatherhood wasn't for him when the child was old enough to realise he or she wasn't wanted. She would rather raise the baby on her own in a house full of love, than subject it to the childhood she'd had knowing only one parent cared.

As much as she'd told herself she could do everything on her own, having Niccolo in her corner eased a lot of that pressure on her, took away that judgement she would face from the world. It wasn't as big a story, or scandal, for a married princess to be pregnant. The timing they could deal with later, but she was sure it wouldn't cause as much of a fuss if she was married to who the world assumed was the baby's father.

That was a big tick in the pro column for a marriage she hadn't expected. If Niccolo was willing to be the father Stefan couldn't be, this baby would have the security of two parents. They didn't have to love each other to make a good team and provide a stable home to raise this child.

Of course, this marriage meant she might never have another long-term relationship with anyone else. It was a big sacrifice, yet one she'd be willing to make for the sake of her child. At least then she wouldn't be under any pressure to meet someone else and go through all the associated heartache when she was inevitably found wanting in some way. She could live without the rejection and humiliation that seemed to come with relationships, both hers and that of her parents. Arranged marriages sometimes worked and she reckoned they had a fighting chance when they both knew what they were getting into from the start. It wouldn't hurt that they appeared to like each other too.

'You can put my name on the birth certificate if it will put your mind at ease,' Niccolo replied finally. 'I know what it's like to be treated as a burden and I would never inflict that on anyone else. If I'm in this marriage, I'm in this family, and I promise I will be the best father I can be.'

'Thank you, that means a lot. I suppose this marriage of convenience would at least be one I've had a part in arranging. It appears you've got the family's approval too, so I think you've bagged yourself a wife.' She wouldn't put it past her grandfather to push her into another marriage to suit him better if he knew the real circumstances. He surely wasn't so progressive that he would continue to champion her as the next head of the monarchy as a single mother. At least she and Niccolo had some sort of bond, even if it had transpired because they were victims of circumstance instead of naturally occurring.

Gaia held out her hand for Niccolo to shake and seal the deal. If he was really willing to risk everything to help her out it would be remiss of her not to accept his offer of marriage.

It was only when she experienced that tingle through her whole body again when he touched her, reminding her of everything he'd made her feel when they'd danced together, that she thought she might live to regret her decision.

'So what do we do now?' Niccolo was so far out of his depth his feet were no longer touching the ground. Yes, he'd seen marriage as their only viable option out of this mess but now he was taking on a fatherhood role he'd never anticipated.

A family hadn't been something he'd seen for himself due to his own troubled upbringing. It was the thought of repeating history and turning into his own father which had held him back, along with his inability to commit to a partner. Now there was a baby in need of a loving, supportive father, he knew he had to step up. He couldn't live with the picture Christina had painted of him, even in his own head. Somewhere deep down he knew he was capable of love, or else it wouldn't have hurt so much losing his mother. All he had to do was access those feelings to prove to Gaia, the baby, and himself that he could be a good man, and father. Hopefully he wasn't leaving himself vulnerable at the same time.

It was going to come as one hell of a surprise to Ana, since she'd witnessed their first meeting only a matter of hours ago. Albeit a pleasant one. She would see the publicity of his upcoming nuptials to a princess as a cash and career windfall no doubt, yet he wasn't even sure he'd be able to continue working once they were married. He made a mental note to query that at a later date, though he was sure he'd have a list of other questions by then too. All the other things he hadn't considered when he'd leapt in to save Gaia's reputation. He didn't regret it, he simply wished he'd taken some more time to mull over the consequences of his actions.

Gaia's eyes were wide, as though she was gradually coming out of the same dream he was currently trying to process. 'I don't know… I suppose we wait for instructions. They'll be making all of the wedding arrangements, so I'm not sure how much input we'll have.'

'Hmm. I wouldn't say I'm an expert on marriage but I know a bride usually wants her say on the dress and the décor, at least.' None of this was fair, on either of them, but Niccolo didn't think Gaia should be denied the simplest of joys to be had in this day, no matter that the circumstances were less than ideal.

She shrugged. 'It doesn't seem that important in the scheme of things.'

Niccolo hated to see her so downhearted when he was doing everything within his power to make her happy. He didn't know why that had suddenly become so important to him, only that it had started the moment they'd met. In that second in the line-up at the premiere, there had been a spark of recognition between them that hadn't yet been extinguished, and he knew he would do anything to save a like-minded soul from the misery he'd suffered these past years.

He placed his hands gently on her shoulders and felt her slump beneath his fingertips, as though that simple contact was enough to ease some of the tension in her body. It only seemed natural then to hug her, to let her know that he had her back. Something he wished he'd had when he'd needed it most.

'Hey, you matter, Gaia,' he said and pulled her close, wrapping her in his arms as though she were a burrito. Holding her so tight she couldn't fall apart.

Her little sniff as she buried her head against his chest was the only indication she gave of any emotion, something he was sure she'd been programmed to withhold on account of her high-profile status. He could relate on a certain level when he'd held back for so many years. Still, it was nice to feel wanted, needed, and to provide some comfort in return.

With everything that had gone on with his ex he'd questioned his own character. Perhaps what he was doing for Gaia was to ease his conscience about the way he'd treated girlfriends past, an atonement for the man they thought him to be. Deep down he knew he was as vulnerable as everyone else, possibly more so. He had to be careful that by giving so much of himself to protect Gaia, he didn't leave himself unprotected. Especially when he was about to become part of the royal family, scrutinised more than ever, and accountable to more than himself. He had to be strong for them both because he didn't want Gaia to become overwhelmed by her situation the way he had, not with a baby on the way.

Yes, that was added pressure on him too, becoming a stand-in father for a baby that wasn't his, with a wife he'd never intended to have, but he was sure they'd come up with some way to be happy. Despite the trouble which had followed, that short time they'd had together alone had been exhilarating. He'd felt more like the old Niccolo, carefree and uninhibited by the lies which had dogged him for so long. Gaia never once gave him the impression that she doubted his character, putting her trust in him to lead her in that now controversial dance. The only person since his public character assassination to have faith in him, other than Ana, who was paid to remain by his side. He owed it to Gaia and this child to show them the same support.

When she gave a contented sigh and he was tempted to carry her off, away from everything causing her stress, Niccolo knew it was time to let go of her. Before they got too comfortable.

He peeled her away and held her at arm's length for both of their sakes. 'What did you always dream of for your wedding?'

'Well, it wasn't a maternity dress and a fake fiancé. No offence.' She gave him a wobbly smile that made him want to hug her all the more.

'None taken. It's not exactly the life either of us had planned, but let's make the best of it, eh?' Niccolo wanted to do something to take her mind off whatever her family were currently conspiring for her future, and for them both to have a little fun.

'What do you suggest? A joint stag and hen party?' She arched an eyebrow at him, a smirk playing on her lips when she knew even the thought of it would get them into more trouble.

'I'm not sure either of us is up for a party limousine and strippers.' Perhaps in a different life, before his very public downfall, he might have considered that a good night, minus the impending nuptials. Now, however, nothing about that appealed to him. He'd settle for a quiet drink in a local pub, not that it would be an option for them.

Gaia pouted. 'Spoilsport.'

'I mean, you're a princess, in which case I imagine you can order anything you like, so getting a baby-oiled, out-of-work dancer in a loincloth should be a piece of cake.'

She took a step back, looking him up and down so overtly it was making him self-conscious.

'What?'

'I was just thinking…you can dance, not currently working, and I'm sure I have a bottle of baby oil somewhere…' That mischievous glint in her eye, the smirk which had morphed into a full-blown smile, and even the sound of her laughing at his expense, made her seem more like the Gaia he'd first met.

'You know, I was once offered the lead in a film about male strippers. I did learn a few moves before the funding fell through.'

'Uh-huh?' The way she was looking at him only made him want to carry on with the flirtatious exchange. To make them forget the serious business of marriage and babies in favour of some fun.

'I can do a full body roll that could make those dollar bills rain down.'

'I'm sure you could.' The breathless reply called straight to his ego, and other parts of him keen to show off.

He began to hum the sexy tune he'd used to get into character and slowly undid his tie, whipping it out from his collar, whirling it like a lasso, then hooking it around Gaia's neck to pull her closer. Her giggle only encouraged him.

He bit his lip and popped open the top button of his shirt, before sliding his hand provocatively down the front of his body. Gaia covered her eyes in mock horror, only to peek out again in time to see him shimmy one arm out of his jacket.

'Gaia, don't forget you have that visit to the local women's group later.' Princess Amara walked in again, took one look at the scene, tutted and turned on her heel.

Once they'd got over the embarrassment of her witnessing their little flirtation, both he and Gaia began to laugh.

He shrugged his jacket back on, did up his buttons and retrieved his tie.

'Talk about timing,' he joked to diffuse that sexual tension which had crept in between them once more.

He hated everything about the circumstances which conspired to quash that spirit he so greatly admired in her and vowed to do everything he could to keep that smile on her face. Even if the way she was looking at him called to that primal part of him that wanted to pick up where they'd left off that night at the premiere, before the rest of the world had crashed in and ruined the moment. Every now and then he wondered what might have happened if they'd been left alone with that obvious chemistry sparking between them.

That in itself was enough to concern him. Even in wanting to explore those feelings he was leaving himself vulnerable again, losing control to his libido at a time when he needed it most. He wanted to be the loyal husband Gaia needed, and the supportive father the baby deserved. To do that he had to access emotions he'd locked away, but with that he ran the risk of letting them affect him too deeply. He had to shut down this attraction now—it couldn't run alongside the emotional connection they already had; past relationships told him that. It was sex or companionship; the two things couldn't cohabit in his world without his risking getting hurt.

They'd been forced together into a marriage they both hoped would save their reputations. They couldn't afford to give in to temptation and let a blaze of passion carry them away for a short time. That was how most of his relationships went, until that spark eventually died and he knew it was time to move on because there was nothing beyond that physical attraction to continue a relationship. This time he'd made a promise, a commitment, to support Gaia, and he wasn't going to let his libido get in the way of that.

'That definitely would've been a box-office hit,' Gaia insisted as he dressed.

'I think my dancing days are over,' he said, his voice dangerously gruff simply thinking about what could have been.

'Shame,' she teased.

'I think,' he pulled his phone from his pocket, looking for a distraction from the feelings he wasn't supposed to have, 'we should have an afternoon planning our wedding. Even if it doesn't happen, I'd like to know what you would've wanted.'

She tilted her head to one side, watching him with scepticism as though waiting for him to tell her he was joking. To prove he was serious, he did an image search on his phone for wedding dresses and picked out the most hideous one he could find.

'What about this one? I think the peach chiffon would suit you and that bonnet is just crying out for a shepherd's crook accessory.'

Her laugh was a welcome sound in a place he wasn't sure had heard much of it recently.

'Okay, okay, crazy man, we'll play make-believe for the afternoon, but only because I'm afraid you'll order this and expect me to wear it.' She grabbed his phone as she walked past him on her way to the sofa.

Niccolo took a seat beside her and relaxed watching Gaia come back to life, picking out her favourite flowers and showing him her likes and dislikes, letting him get to know her better. Something he looked forward to but also dreaded when he didn't need any further reason to like her.

Niccolo had gone home to start putting his affairs in order before he officially became part of the royal establishment. Leaving her alone to try and make sense of what had happened over the course of one afternoon—dropping the baby bombshell which had haunted her for so long, followed by a surprise proposal and an offer of a father to her baby.

She was lying on her bed replaying the events of the day and wondering how she'd got so lucky by running into Niccolo. His generosity of spirit was the only thing helping her get through something which could easily have ruined her life. She just hoped he would get as much out of the deal as she should.

Marriage provided her with someone to accompany her on her royal duties, a sounding board for her problems and ideas. It gave her someone other than her parents to turn to in good times and bad. Most of all, she would have a partner to share parenthood with. She didn't have to be on her own any more.

It was ironic that he was the only one who actually felt like family to Gaia at a time when she should have been relying on her mother's support now more than ever. Though currently her relationship with her parents could be called strained at the very least. She knew she was a disappointment to everyone, but Niccolo's intervention had helped to reduce the size of the mess to hopefully manageable levels. It wasn't an ideal situation but preferable to the one she'd believed herself to be in before his proposal.

After dropping the baby bombshell in front of her family she'd just wanted to hide away. Niccolo had taken charge and turned the whole thing on its head so they were now planning a wedding instead of trying to manage another scandal. She would probably have been content to let everyone else organise the big day around her as if she wasn't really a part of it. In her mind she just had to show up, let them dress her, parade her in front of the media, say 'I do', and disappear again until it was time for her to step into her grandfather's footsteps. It wasn't as though any of it was real. Even if Niccolo's impromptu sexy dance had made her experience very real feelings. Namely lust. Her mother's interruption had probably been for the best before they'd got carried away, but she couldn't help thinking she'd been denied a very special performance.

Despite the circumstances, Niccolo was doing his best to try and make the experience enjoyable for her. As though this wedding was for real.

She supposed it was in a way, when it would be the only one she was likely to have.

This afternoon he'd got her excited about what she would be wearing, looking at wedding dresses and getting to know her style. Something she supposed she should have been doing with a best friend who would be supporting her on the day as chief bridesmaid, but Gaia didn't have anyone close enough to do that with. It was only now she realised how lonely the life of a princess was. The price she paid for her privileged position in society.

Now she had Niccolo, she had someone to talk to who gave her a hug when she needed one, and who ordered mocktails and cake samples to cheer her up. He'd become her best friend in the short time she'd known him. Exactly what was needed in a husband. Except this was supposed to be a marriage of convenience, a career move and a way to save face.

She wasn't supposed to be falling for him.

CHAPTER FIVE

'I'M JUST PLAYING a part,' Niccolo told himself as he waited at the end of the aisle facing the ornate stained-glass window casting candy-coloured shadows across the altar.

He hoped he wouldn't go to hell for trying to do the right thing.

Sweat beaded on his freshly shaved top lip. *He* wasn't actually marrying a princess in front of the whole world and accepting responsibility for a baby that wasn't his. That was Niccolo Pernici's latest starring role.

Except when he cast his eye over his shoulder it felt very much as though it was him everyone was staring at. His father and his latest partner were there too, beaming at him. He'd been forced to invite him at the behest of the royal advisors and Gaia's family to avoid any scandal about a family rift. They'd all agreed that, by giving him a prime spot and keeping him sweet, it would steer him away from trying to make money selling salacious stories about his son. Niccolo wasn't sure that accord would last for ever, but he had called a truce with his father for the sake of his new family. This was the ultimate privilege for his father. He believed his son's need to have him back in his life was as genuine as this wedding. As did Gaia's family and the minister about to perform the ceremony.

He deserved an award for this level of acting, or a prison sentence for fraud.

No movie premiere or red-carpeted event could ever have prepared him for the worldwide interest in this ceremony. The security, the press coverage and the sheer number of people lining the streets to wish them well was overwhelming even to someone used to being in the spotlight. With any luck, once the wedding was over, interest in them as a couple would die down.

In their position it wasn't going to be possible to live a 'normal' life but he knew they both wanted one without their every move being watched and criticised. Though today was not that day.

The cathedral organ began to play, the pipes filling the air with their dramatic vibrations. He heard the communal shifting of people in the pews and a murmuring of wonder, and instinctively knew Gaia had made her entrance.

It seemed an eternity waiting for her to come to his side and remind him he wasn't doing this alone. They were in this mess together.

The anticipation was killing him, waiting for his bride-to-be. If he could just see her face he would be less tempted to run out of here. There would have been tremendous pressure on him no matter who he was marrying, but he was joining the royal family based on a lie. The fallout of that secret ever being revealed would be monumental, and the very thought of being exposed had his heart thumping so hard he worried it might crack through his chest.

He had to see Gaia to know it was all worth it to prevent the baying press tearing them both to shreds. She didn't deserve that any more than he had and, being honest, he hoped this marriage would benefit his career as much as his reputation too. It had been made clear to him that the royal family weren't supposed to work in normal jobs alongside their duties, but his wasn't any run-of-the-mill, nine-to-five career. They'd agreed he could take roles which didn't bring the family into disrepute or interfere with his royal duties, so he would be limited. But he expected after their wedding was beamed across the world that his star would shine brightly in the land of celebrity once more. He'd be a fool not to capitalise on that in case this all ended tomorrow and he was left with nothing again.

In turn for helping boost his profile, he'd done what he could to make Gaia happy thus far.

He thought she should have had some input into her wedding day as though it were the real thing. Getting to learn her likes and dislikes, laughing at some of the outlandish creations proposed to her, eating their way through a ton of cake he'd managed to get delivered to the palace, they'd become close. That hadn't been part of the deal but now it felt as though they were in a private club, a dastardly duo in cahoots to dupe the world.

He glanced back again and a shy smile from his glowing bride was the confirmation he needed to see this through. It would all be worth it if he could make her happy, prove to himself and everyone else that he wasn't the coldhearted so-and-so his ex had painted him as.

'You look beautiful,' he whispered, uncaring if he was breaking any sort of etiquette because it was true. He needed to say it and she needed to hear it.

'Thank you,' she mouthed back, appearing every bit as nervous as he.

Niccolo gulped as the minister addressed the congregation, ready to perform the ceremony.

Whatever happened from here, they were in this together, bound by secrets and lies for ever.

Gaia couldn't quite believe they were doing this. That they were actually getting married. Niccolo had carried out his promise. The first man in her life she could remember doing so, though only time would tell if that would last.

In the days since the proposal and the hub-bub around the announcement she'd expected him to pull out when he came to his senses and realised what he was getting into. Yet he'd been there for her every wobbly step of the way, re-assuring her that things would work out, and banishing that cloud of shame and worry which had hung over her since seeing that positive pregnancy test. She'd come to trust him and was putting her faith in him not to do the dirty on her like her exes or her own father. Men who'd treated her as though her feelings didn't matter, and rejected her when they grew tired of having her around.

The knowledge that she was lying not only to her parents, but also to the whole world, with this marriage, still weighed heavily on her heart. When she'd shared that burden with Niccolo, his answer was to remind her that she was doing this for the future of the country. This marriage was to provide stability not only for the baby, but also for the monarchy as a whole. It might not survive another scandal, but this wedding could bring the country together to wish them well. As proved by the thousands of people waving outside and watching this ceremony live on the television. They didn't realise how much more there was to Niccolo Pernici the movie star, and she was privileged that she did.

'You may kiss the bride.' The minister brought her back into the present, facing Niccolo, eyes wide with disbelief at the situation and the fact they had both gone ahead with this.

It would look odd if they didn't show some affection, so she leaned in for the first kiss with her husband.

The rest of the congregation faded into her peripheral vision as she focused on Niccolo. His eyes centred on her lips, she parted them in anticipation of his touch. He cupped her face in his large palms and her eyes fluttered shut. She wanted to believe this was real, that her handsome groom had agreed to spend the rest of his life with her, raising their baby, out of love. That when his lips met hers it was because he wanted to kiss her and that he was enjoying it as much as she was, regardless of the brevity of the intimacy.

Then the moment was over, the witnesses clapping them as they made their way back down the aisle. Her mother and grandfather nodded their approval. They even looked happy. She offered them a quivering smile in return, guilt darkening her soul.

Despite the people lining their path, offering their congratulations, Gaia felt totally alone. Then Niccolo caught her little finger with his, linking them together to remind her he was right there with her. That small gesture seemed an even greater one than saying, 'I do.'

'If I'd known my son was dating the future Queen I would have asked for a tax exemption,' Niccolo's father joked to the sound of forced laughter from the guests listening to his cringe-worthy speech.

Niccolo prayed for this to be over. Listening to all the speeches praising them and celebrating their love had been excruciating. If he'd had his way they would have been on the first flight out of the country after the ceremony to avoid prolonging the agony, but that idea had been vetoed by 'the management'. In the end both he and Gaia had to accept that, to convince everyone of the authenticity of the wedding, they would have to treat it exactly as any other royal wedding and put up with the ensuing formalities.

Gaia rested her hand on his thigh under the table, letting him know that she was hating this as much as he was, but there for him. It was obvious they were both suffering from nerves, anxiety stealing their appetite in the face of the sumptuous feast laid on for them.

'Are you sure you wouldn't like a glass of champagne?' Gaia's mother asked.

'No, thank you.' With all the secrets he was keeping it was necessary to keep a clear head so he didn't let any slip out. There was too much at stake to over-indulge on his wedding day. Although he wished he'd had some Dutch courage when it came to making his speech.

He got to his feet as he was introduced by the MC and waited for the applause to die down before he spoke. In preparation for the day he'd decided to treat it like a scene in one of his movies, saying things that would have been expected from someone of his new standing, thanking the royal family for accepting him. All the while knowing it was something which had been forced upon them. In other circumstances he wasn't sure they would even have contemplated letting a movie star join their ranks. When it was a choice between that and leaving the future Queen as a single mother, he guessed he was the lesser of two evils.

Every now and then he threw a glance at Gaia, but she kept her head down, avoiding his gaze. It was only when he addressed her personally that she gazed up at him, her cheeks pink from his adoration. Those parts of his speech were the only genuine words that came out of his mouth.

'You're a wonderful woman, Gaia, and I'm glad I met you. Here's to a long and happy marriage.' He raised his glass and toasted their future along with everyone else in the room, not missing the tremble of Gaia's bottom lip as he turned to her.

'I meant every word. I'm not going into this marriage lightly. I'll work every day to try and bring some joy back into your life,' he whispered. They both deserved a break, and if fate insisted on putting obstacles in their way he would double his efforts to get over them. It was in both of their interests to make this marriage a success and he'd do everything in his power to make that happen.

Gaia reached over and hugged him, dropping a kiss on his cheek to a chorus of 'Aw…' from the watching crowd. He knew she hadn't done it for show, it was a gesture, like the leg pat, to show solidarity during this most difficult performance of his life. Her touch shouldn't make him want this to be real, anticipating their honeymoon as a chance to physically express his feelings in private. Making love hadn't been part of the deal. They hadn't even discussed it. Now, knowing they were about to spend time away alone, it was all he could think about.

The end of the speeches couldn't come too soon for Gaia. It wasn't easy listening to lies made up for the guests caught up in the romance of the day. They hadn't come solely from her and Niccolo either. Her father had ignored his invitation, and, while she hoped it was because he didn't want to take away the focus from the newlyweds, it was more likely he didn't care she was getting married. To save face her grandfather had stepped in and given his speech about how proud of her they all were and how much they were looking forward to having Niccolo as part of the family. All lies. Just as much a show for the audience as the ceremony had been.

It was Niccolo's words she had taken to heart, his promise that she would be happy. Oh, how she wished that to be true. Crucially that hadn't been part of their deal, but if he was willing to genuinely be a husband to her beyond appearances' sake, it was more than she could have dreamed of. It gave her a flickering ember of hope inside that some day she might be happy again, not simply existing.

That feeling was further stoked when they took to the floor for their first dance. As they swayed together on the floor, Niccolo making her look good as he led her in a traditional waltz, she believed this was more than a business deal to him.

'Thank you for a wonderful day,' she mumbled into his neck in her trance-like state.

Her chest was pressed so close to his that his laugh reverberated through both of their bodies. 'You're welcome. Although I think next time we should go to Vegas.'

Niccolo made her smile even in the most trying of times. 'I mean it. Despite the circumstances I'm glad you're the man I'm marrying.'

'Well, thank you. There's no other princess I'd rather be saving,' he whispered into her ear, making the hairs on the back of her neck stand to attention, and goose-pimples ripple across her skin.

His apparent affection for her, combined with all the amazing things he'd done to get them here, was an aphrodisiac she didn't need when they were about to go on a sex-free honeymoon.

'I thought we'd never get to be on our own,' Niccolo said as he closed the blinds in their honeymoon villa.

'You'd better get used to it,' Gaia sighed, brushing away the rose petals so she could lie back on the massive bed. She appreciated the gesture, but in this case it wasn't necessary to set the mood, along with the champagne and burning candles. The chocolates she pulled closer, sure she would have a need for those later.

They'd agreed on taking the trip more because they knew they'd need a break from reality than to keep up the public façade.

'It's a shame I'll never be nominated for any awards after this.' He helped himself to one of the chocolate-covered strawberries sitting amongst the harvest of fruit on the huge glass table.

A generous bite later and she was watching the juice squirt over his bottom lip, his tongue sweeping out to lick it away. Clearly her hormones were raging out of control, making her crave more than the sweetness of the chocolate and the juiciness of the berry.

'Would you like some?'

Yes, please, she thought, watching him saunter over to the bed, his shirt unbuttoned and showing off his taut, tanned chest. It was one thing seeing him practically naked on the big screen but totally hotter to have him here in the bedroom with her. The irony wasn't lost on Gaia that she was crushing on her own husband but she was sure it was simply because he had shown her a kindness. Not only was he prepared to play father to a baby that wasn't his, but he'd made it through the pomp and ceremony of the wedding ceremony with a smile on his face for her.

She'd never felt as though she had a place in the world until today. Her ex hadn't wanted her, and neither had her father, and she was never meant to step into his shoes, so this new path to her reign was alien to her. There was no way of testing how much the public respected her, and she worried when she did come to the throne the only place she was comfortable was with Niccolo. She didn't have to pretend who she was around him. He was aware she was a frightened, pregnant, jilted, reluctant heiress to the throne and he was still here, feeding her chocolate-dipped strawberries.

She took a bite, savouring the tang of the juice and the bitter sweetness of the coating. Niccolo caught the small piece of chocolate clinging to her lip with his thumb, pausing before sucking it off. Gaia wondered if he was thinking about the tender kiss they'd shared at the altar before he'd walked away again.

She was being silly, getting carried away by the romance of the day and the location of their Bali honeymoon. Some time together realising what they'd got themselves into would surely knock any such notions out of her head. Her father, along with all her previous partners, had promised her the world at one time or another. Only to ditch her when someone more exciting came along. She was sure, despite appearances, that Niccolo would do the same at some point. He hadn't committed to her personally, or sworn his undying love, so there was more chance of that happening than she wanted to think about.

'I'm sorry things moved so fast. I'm aware your offer of marriage was to get me out of a sticky situation with my family and you likely never imagined you'd end up here.'

'You're right. If I'd known I'd have to spend a week on an island with a beautiful woman to convince the world we were a couple I would have demanded a pay check.' The teasing did the job of reminding her this was a business arrangement and a rushed one at that.

The family might have insisted on Niccolo signing prenups and non-disclosure agreements in case the marriage ended, so the money and family secrets were protected, but they hadn't made their own personal arrangement legally binding. There would be nothing to stop Niccolo walking away at any time and they hadn't laid down any ground rules about what they expected from one another.

'It's not too late for us to put something down in writing about our personal arrangement. I'll understand if you'd like to get some legal advice on the matter.' They hadn't thought this through properly. All she'd seen was a way out of her personal crisis, a temporary solution to a permanent problem.

In hindsight, a marriage based solely on circumstance could bring on its own set of problems.

'I don't think that's necessary. I mean, we can do that if it would make you more comfortable, but I'm happy to take one day at a time.' Niccolo popped the cork on the bottle of champagne chilling in an ice bucket and slurped the escaping fizz before decanting into two glass flutes.

She probably would have been happier with a signed contract saying he'd never leave or hurt her, but that was wishful thinking. It was pure good fortune on her part that he'd come this far with her.

'I guess I'm wondering what will happen when the baby gets here. It's not going to be easy for you.'

'I went into this with my eyes open, Gaia. I'll be here for you and the baby. It's not as though you conned me into marrying you for love. I suppose this was a career move of sorts for both of us.' He handed her a glass of champagne, but even if she hadn't been pregnant she didn't feel much like celebrating. It was literally only Niccolo preventing her from spiralling into a dark abyss of despair due to her past mistakes. She could only hope she wasn't making another one.

Loving her wasn't one of the conditions of their deal. She needed him to keep telling her this was a business arrangement in case she started to believe in her own fairy-tale ending.

'Just a sip to celebrate our nuptials,' he said, assuming her reluctance was because of the baby.

Rather than give him extra reasons to fret about their future too, she accepted the glass.

'To us.' Niccolo clinked his champagne to hers.

'To us,' she said, forcing a sip and a smile, praying they could make this work for the baby's sake if nothing else.

'So, what are the sleeping arrangements?'

Gaia spluttered, shooting champagne bubbles up her nose. 'I—er—hadn't thought about that. As you say, we should probably take one day at a time and just see how things go between us.'

She didn't think sex was part of the deal but

she supposed men had needs and some day she might too. They didn't have to be married in name only if they found each other acceptable in that way. It would be preferable to thinking about Niccolo with another woman.

She watched his eyebrows lift skyward.

'That's…uh…' He cleared his throat and took another sip of champagne. 'I meant for tonight. There's only one bed and we might raise suspicion if I sleep out on the beach on our honeymoon.'

Gaia wanted to throw herself back onto the mattress in the hope that she would sink into it and be suffocated by the nest of ornate cushions placed around her. It showed where her mind was compared to his when she was thinking about making love to someone who was still pretty much a stranger to her, despite outward appearances.

One step at a time, she told herself.

They were still getting to know one another and goodness knew what he thought of her now, pregnant and practically throwing herself at him.

'Yes. Of course.' Ugh, now he knew she'd thought about sharing a bed with him. The fact that she was open to the idea might scare him away altogether.

'Don't get me wrong, I'm not opposed to the

idea, Princess. It's just, well, we don't know each other very well.'

'You're on the floor, buddy.'

Even though she'd embarrassed herself, she appreciated that Niccolo was comfortable enough to tease her like this. It made things easier.

He gave a bow. 'M'lady was always going to have the bed. I might take the couch instead though. I'm not sure my back could hold out on the floor.'

She gave him the side-eye as she flounced by on her way to the bathroom clutching her nightwear. The whisper of his clothes being removed and the sound of his belt hitting the floor turned her mouth dry as she imagined him getting naked behind her.

She closed the bathroom door and faced her flushed face in the mirror. It was hormone-related, nothing to do with the sight waiting for her out there. She splashed her face with cold water and unpicked the pins holding her hair in its neat prison. Shaking her hair out felt like finally shedding her public princess image. Apart from the fact that she was still wearing the restrictive tailored ivory and black contrast dress she'd changed into before they'd boarded their flight. In hindsight she should have probably chosen something more comfortable, like elasticated lounge wear, for the journey but she was still in that mindset of trying to look good for him. It was ridiculous dressing up in an attempt to impress him when none of this marriage was based on love or attraction, but part of her still needed the validation.

Now that neediness was coming back to bite her on the bum. She reached behind her back to undo the zip to discover too late she needed an extra hand. No matter what shape she contorted herself into she couldn't quite reach the high neck on her own.

Swallowing her pride and whatever other emotion had surged forward upon seeing Niccolo lying half naked under a sheet on the chaise longue, she asked for his help.

'Sure.' He jumped up, letting the cotton sheet slide away to reveal most of his muscular form, save for the area covered by his black boxers, thank goodness.

She spun around, afraid her eyes would linger too long on any specific part of his anatomy, and waited for assistance.

Niccolo carefully lifted her hair and draped it over her shoulder before unzipping the dress in one long, languid motion, his knuckles intimately grazing along her spine. She thought about how it would feel to have his lips follow the same path, to touch her bare skin just as softly and intimately as his fingers.

Gaia bit her lip, attempting to stave off that aching need she was sure would follow that brief connection. It happened every time he touched her. A feeling she was grateful to still experience, yet saddened her to know that there could never be anything more. She didn't want anything to spoil this new chance she'd been given to prove herself as a better daughter, mother and future Queen.

'Thanks.' Her voice was thick with something more than gratitude. This was beyond simply unsticking her from a dress, he was awaking every single erogenous zone with one glancing touch. Even if she was sure a night in Niccolo's arm would be glorious when the slightest brush of his hand melted her, she wasn't naïve enough to think it could solve all her problems, or even last.

'I'm—er—sure you can manage the rest,' he mumbled, stepping back to break the physical connection between them. If he hadn't felt that same pull of attraction he wouldn't have had the need to back away so awkwardly he'd nearly fallen backwards over the settee. But Niccolo had the presence of mind to see the possibility of more as a mistake, ending the frisson before it had a chance to fully take a hold of them both. At least one of them was still in control of their faculties.

She scurried back to the bathroom and slipped on the midnight-blue silk chemise she'd bought specially for the night. Niccolo might not be her lover but she didn't want him to see her in the usual comfy pyjamas she wore to bed. It was their honeymoon after all.

It was tempting to make a dash for the bed instead of giving him time to watch her walk across the room when she was self-conscious about her newly changing body. Judging by the look on his face when she walked by, she might as well have been naked, and she did find some satisfaction as he covered himself with the sheet again.

'We'll have to come up with a better arrangement when we get home,' he growled as she climbed into bed.

'It isn't unheard of to have separate rooms. Though not straight after our wedding. The staff do gossip.'

'The staff,' he snorted. 'I'm not sure I'll ever get used to that.'

'You'll have to, since you'll likely never be alone again.' It was ironic that someone who'd longed for privacy her entire life had never felt lonelier after discovering she was pregnant. At least until Niccolo had tangoed into her life.

'I'm not sure if that's heartening or depressing.'

'What do you think?'

'It can't be all bad. There aren't any bills to pay…people who will do anything you say and clean up after you. It must be like a holiday camp.'

'If you don't mind people watching your every move, can't have any sort of normal life, and have to be careful of every word you utter…yes, it's a joy.' She was aware he was trying to wind her up, to lighten her mood. It was his default setting. Except the restrictions placed upon her because of her lineage were the reason she was spending her wedding night in bed alone with the man pretending to love her sleeping across the room. Given the chance, she wouldn't have chosen this and it astounded her every day that he had.

'You make it sound like prison but, since I'm an outsider, I'm allowed to make waves. I know there are rules but we need space to live our own lives. When we get back there are going to be changes. I don't want you to be unhappy. You've been through enough and it's my job as your partner to protect you, Gaia. I'm not about to start a revolution but I am going to be the best husband and father I can. I take my responsibilities seriously. Now, goodnight, Wife.'

'Goodnight, Husband.'

Niccolo turned out the light, leaving Gaia with a smile on her face. For the first time since peeing on that life-changing plastic stick she fell into a deep, peaceful slumber. Safe in the knowledge that Niccolo was there to keep the nightmares away.

Niccolo listened to the sound of Gaia's steady breathing as she slept. He was glad he'd been able to reassure her things were going to work out, even if he was doubting it himself. It was a lot to take on, marrying a pregnant princess, regardless of its being a marriage of convenience. At least in terms of their careers. Logistically he wasn't certain how convenient it was going to be living under a microscope with a bunch of strangers, any of whom could uncover their secret and run to the press at any time.

He did take his responsibilities seriously, which was why he'd never had any intention of getting married or starting a family. Naively, in his gallant rescue of Gaia's honour, he'd believed that it would be a straightforward transaction. That no emotional involvement would make this relatively easy. Once they'd fooled the world that they were in love they could carry on with their lives.

Now he was beginning to realise what he'd signed up for. It wasn't the lack of privacy which was bothering him—he'd survived the past year in that environment—but the messy complication of emotions.

He'd stupidly convinced himself that night they'd been caught in a moment of flirtation had been nothing more than that. An acknowledgement of mutual attraction. Watching her walk down the aisle had confirmed that attraction and tonight was further proof that he wanted her.

It was proving more difficult than he'd imagined to separate his emotions from a relationship in this instance when that attraction was already so clearly there between them. He was destined for an uncomfortable night, not only remembering the breathtaking sight of her body sheathed in silk but also the warmth of her skin and the hitch in her breath when he'd touched her. All topped off with the less than chaste kiss they'd shared in church. He already had feelings for her. Not a good idea when embarking on a fake royal romance.

With a baby also in the picture things would go from bad to worse when he cared about Gaia. Despite not being the father he was bound to have some affection for the child because it was hers and because the whole world was under the impression he was the father.

The child was going to grow up believing him

to be its father too and he didn't want to replicate his own parent, distant and distracted. Ready or not, he was embarking on a life of domesticity with this strange new family.

The trouble being that success as a family man involved showing feelings and expressing emotions. Something his last partner had fought so hard to get him to show they'd almost gone to court. He couldn't be sure if the past year had changed him as a person but he would be whoever Gaia needed him to be to prevent her from going through the same pain he'd suffered.

A promise had been made, a deal done, and now he had to find a way to live with it. Even if it meant keeping his true feelings to himself.

CHAPTER SIX

THEY'D SPENT THE first few days of their fake honeymoon winding down from the stress of their whirlwind wedding. Breakfast together was a quiet affair on the balcony every morning, followed by lazy afternoons lying by the pool. Other than that it seemed as though they'd been trying to keep their distance from one another, despite their close quarters. Niccolo would pop his ear buds in, stretch out on the sun lounger and close his eyes, listening to music and effectively blocking her out. Gaia buried herself in the stack of books she'd brought with her so they didn't have to make small talk.

At night Niccolo waited until after she'd gone to bed before he bunked down on the sofa. He probably would have stayed out in the lounge if it weren't for the busy staff who seemed to be ever present. Although she should have been pleased they hadn't had a repeat of their awkward wedding night, she did stay awake every night hoping to catch a glimpse of Niccolo getting ready for bed. She put it down to her hormones that she was lusting after him when anything more than that spelt trouble. Especially when they were already dodging acknowledging that chemistry she knew was currently keeping them both awake at night.

'Can I get you a drink, sir?' The sound of their pretty, young housekeeper filtered across the pool as she approached Niccolo.

He lifted his sunglasses onto his head and gave her his full attention. 'What have you got for me, Cassandra?'

She began to run through a list of cocktails on offer when Niccolo reached out a hand to stop her. 'Why don't you surprise me?' he asked with a smile.

'I'll make you something special, Mr Niccolo. Something strong and sexy. Like you.' The over-familiar member of staff had the audacity to wink at Gaia's new husband before she sashayed away.

Worse still, Niccolo was smiling, encouraging the outrageous behaviour.

Gaia huffed out a breath as she turned the page of her book with such force she almost tore the corner. Still, she held her tongue. It shouldn't matter to her if the hired help was flirting with him, or that he was enjoying it, when their relationship was fake. They'd agreed their marriage was in name only and she had no right to be jealous. Except he looked so good lying over there, his swim shorts riding low on his hips, a drop of sweat travelling between the valley of his pectoral muscles over his taut belly and into that line of dark hair disappearing into his waistband...

She really shouldn't be watching him so closely, or envying the flirtatious housekeeper with the non-pregnant body. Gaia looked at the slight swell of her tummy encased in an all-in-one black swimsuit and for the first time in her life felt unpretty. She knew the physical changes pregnancy was bringing probably weren't apparent to anyone else yet, but it was what they represented which likely made her less attractive than the ever-attentive Cassandra.

Every time Niccolo looked at her he would see someone who'd trapped him in marriage, see the evidence of another man's baby for which he was going to be responsible. It would be difficult for him not to resent the very sight of her when she'd stripped him of the life he'd had, all because of a silly misunderstanding. Therefore it wasn't surprising he should enjoy a light-hearted exchange with a pretty young woman the way he probably had on a regular basis before Gaia had ruined his life.

A mixture of the sun and her guilt was making her uncomfortably hot and nauseated. With

Cassandra away to mix up Niccolo his special strong and sexy cocktail, he'd lain down again, eyes closed. So Gaia was free to strip off her loose floral cover-all and walk over to the pool without fear that Niccolo was watching, noticing her every flaw.

It was difficult not to think of herself in that way when she'd spent her whole life being analysed by not only the press but also her own family, who demanded perfection in appearance as well as in her every move. Her partners had been the same, expecting her to act like some living doll, beautiful to look at and not much else. They'd fallen for the idea of being with a princess, not realising she was a woman too, with thoughts and feelings which didn't always line up with theirs. But this was supposed to be her new start and it wouldn't work if she couldn't let go of her old way of thinking. It was time she was comfortable in her own skin, regardless if other people approved or not.

The water was cold at first, drawing a short, sharp gasp as she waded down the steps. Then she launched herself into the pool, the water completely enveloping her. She did several laps before turning onto her back and letting her body simply float on the surface, giving the occasional leg kick or circular motion with her hands. There was something freeing about lying here, simply drifting, with the sun on her face, as though she didn't have a care in the world.

That peaceful world came to a shriek-filled end when Niccolo dive-bombed into the pool, showering her with water and leaving her spluttering as she tried to stay afloat.

'Why would you do that?' she asked, wiping the water from her eyes.

'You looked like you needed cooling off,' Niccolo laughed and flicked more water in her direction.

Gaia's immediate reaction was to get her own back, pushing her hand so hard against the surface of the water she caused a wave to break right over his head. He followed up by diving under and pulling her down with him. She struggled out of his grasp and swam away laughing, Niccolo on her tail until they reached the edge of the pool. With one arm on either side of her, he caged her against the tiles. They were grinning at each other as they fought to get their breath back, their legs entwined in the intimacy of the dance. To anyone on the outside they would have looked like typical honeymooners. They were so caught up in having fun that for a split-second Gaia was convinced he was going to kiss her.

'Your drink, Mr Niccolo.' The outside world came calling and the moment was over.

Niccolo immediately swam away and Gaia could only watch with undisguised lust as he got out of the pool, water sluicing down his body, his shorts clinging to his wet skin. He lay face down on the lounger and Cassandra set his drink next to him.

'I think you need more sun cream—let me help you.' Cassandra squeezed out a dollop of lotion into the palm of her hand with no objections coming from Niccolo's quarter, regardless that the oversized parasol was already providing adequate shade.

Gaia couldn't watch any more. She didn't want to witness her husband being massaged by another woman on their honeymoon. Fake relationship or not, she had real feelings for Niccolo which were already proving an inconvenience. She pulled herself up and out of the pool, grabbed her book from the lounger and went back inside, slamming the door shut in a fit of temper. They were supposed to be a married couple. If this was the way he was going to behave, flirting with every woman who crossed his path, while his wife privately seethed with jealousy and lust, her life was going to be more unbearable than ever.

'Thanks, Cassandra, but I can manage.' Niccolo dismissed his attendant, uncomfortable enough without having a stranger rub sun cream into his back.

Gaia had gone back into the room in a fit of pique, highlighting the fact he'd crossed the line. While they'd messed around in the pool it had been easy to forget the reason they were here. In that moment they'd simply been two people enjoying one another's company, not a couple faking a royal romance to save their reputations. She'd looked so happy, like that night when they'd danced together, and once again he'd wanted to kiss her. Thank goodness Cassandra had made a timely entrance, though apparently too late to cover up his wayward thoughts as Gaia had stormed off, clearly upset by his behaviour.

He rolled over and took a sip of the spirit-heavy orange cocktail that made him grimace. With another couple of days of living together like this he had no choice but to go and apologise. Hopefully once they were back in the real world they'd have more space from each other. Though they'd still have to keep up appearances, there would be plenty to keep his mind wandering down dangerous paths. He'd be going into a life of public duty, not to mention the parental responsibility he'd be taking on in another few months. With a schedule of engagements to carry out, not to mention sleepless nights with a new baby, he was sure there wouldn't be much time left for him and Gaia to spend alone. It was probably for the best when this growing attraction and affection towards her was becoming too obvious to ignore.

He took another gulp of alcohol to steel himself before he ventured back inside to beg Gaia's forgiveness.

'Gaia? I'm sorry if I crossed the line back there. I promise from now on to be on my best behaviour,' he called through the closed bedroom door. When there was no reply he let himself into the room, only to find it empty.

He was about to leave and search the rest of the villa when he heard a little cry coming from the bathroom.

'Gaia? Are you okay in there?' He knocked on the door, his heart sinking at the sound of her so upset. All because he couldn't manage to keep his feelings in check. He didn't know what it was about Gaia which made him so reckless when he'd spent years perfecting the art of hiding his emotions. Perhaps it was down to the previous troubled years he'd had when he'd been under tremendous strain. More likely it was because of who Gaia was, a kindred spirit who let him be himself when he was around her, and made it easy for him to let his guard down. Whatever it was, he was going to have to be more careful in the future when emotional entanglement wasn't supposed to be part of their marriage contract.

The sound of a faint sob pricked his conscience again. 'Gaia? I'm coming in, okay?'

He tried the door and gave her a few seconds to react, to tell him to get out, before he stepped inside. The fact that she wasn't yelling at him, demanding some personal space, told him she wasn't herself even before he saw her sitting doubled over on the edge of the bath.

'Something's wrong,' she said, tears and fear glinting in her eyes.

Despite the terror gripping him, Niccolo did his best to remain calm for her sake. It wasn't going to help matters if he got into a panic, even though he was equally as afraid as Gaia that something had happened to the baby.

He knelt down and took her hand. 'What's happened?'

'I was sick, but now there's a crippling pain in my stomach.' She was rubbing her belly as if not only trying to soothe the pain, but also to communicate to her precious baby that she needed it to hold on. If he could get a message in there too, he would. Although becoming a father was something he wasn't particularly looking forward to, especially when the baby wasn't his, he didn't want anything to happen to it. It was part of Gaia, a huge part of his future with her, and he was surprised to discover he was already quite attached to the little life who'd caused so much trouble already.

'Okay. Let's get you into bed and I'll phone for the doctor.' Although they were in a private villa, away from the prying eyes of the rest of the world, they had a full staff on call, including a doctor. No doubt someone handpicked by those who'd arranged their honeymoon who would be very discreet, and likely very expensive. Not something he would usually take advantage of but he wasn't taking any chances where Gaia and the baby were concerned.

With an arm around her back, he guided her over to the bed and helped her under the covers. She was openly sobbing now, her fears that she was losing the baby too much for her to hold back.

'Everything will be all right, Gaia. Just relax.' He did his best to soothe her, even though he was dreading the worst too.

'It might be for the best if I do lose the baby. We could have the marriage annulled and you could go back to your old life, without any obligation to me.' Gaia held his gaze, her jaw set with determination, perhaps steeling herself for the possibly traumatic events ahead.

Niccolo knew it was her fear talking and

pushing him away. Yet it wounded him. He was as invested in this child as much as he was in her. Why else would he have gone into this madcap scheme if not with the goal of protecting them both?

'Don't talk like that, Gaia. You and the baby are both going to be fine. I'll go and call the doctor now.' He turned away before he let those pesky emotions slip out again and said something which could cause irreparable damage to their 'arrangement'.

What he really wanted to tell her was that he was afraid. That this baby was the only thing keeping them together and he didn't want to lose it, or her. But that sentiment wasn't in keeping with the terms of their agreement, or his need to protect his sanity.

It was easier to distance himself from a partner in a relationship when it was just about sex. That wasn't possible in this situation. Even more so because there was a baby involved. And now there was a real possibility of losing it, he might have to deal with that feeling of loss and grief all over again, along with Gaia's.

She was relying on him to help her through this when he was as out of his depth and worried as she was. It was becoming clear that he might not be the robot Christina accused him of being when he was experiencing genuine emotions he hadn't accessed since he was a little boy. And he wasn't sure how to handle it other than trying to quieten them while reassuring Gaia. He needed to keep her calm and he wouldn't do that if he got himself into a flap about what could happen. It was one thing telling her he'd be there for the baby, but he was beginning to realise that meant an extra person in his life to be worried about. He was going to have to find some way to take care of them all without compromising himself any more.

In the meantime, all he could do was hope that this baby was as strong as its mother, and pray neither of them would have to find out what would happen if their future together was cut short. Niccolo wasn't sure he was ready for their marriage, or this family, to be over before it had begun.

Gaia's mouth was dry, her eyes stinging, and her throat raw from crying. It felt as though she was simply lying here waiting to be told the horrible truth, that her baby and the life she'd envisaged was gone. She was in mourning not only for the baby she'd fought so hard to keep, but also for the fledgling relationship she'd embarked on with Niccolo. If something happened she wouldn't blame him if he decided it was the perfect way out of this mess. Her irrational dislike of Cassandra proved she'd already become too attached to him, and if she lost him and the baby she didn't think she'd survive. They were all she had.

She knew she shouldn't be so reliant on him when he'd promised her nothing but a sham marriage, but Niccolo was the only one who understood everything she'd gone through. He was her sole support and confidante. Even now, whilst the doctor was examining her, Niccolo was by her bedside, holding her hand and promising her everything would be all right. When she was looking at him she was more inclined to believe him.

'Have you had any blood spotting?' the doctor asked, removing the cuff from her arm once he'd finished checking her blood pressure.

'No. Just some nausea and cramping.'

He nodded, his glasses resting so low on his nose she feared they'd fall off. 'Your blood pressure is fine but I'll check in on the baby just to put your mind at rest.'

Gaia clutched Niccolo's hand as the doctor squeezed cold gel over her tummy before moving a Doppler foetal heart monitor over the site. She held her breath waiting for confirmation that her baby was still there and Niccolo placed his forehead against hers.

'Whatever happens, I'll be here for you, okay?'

She nodded, biting back the tears, grateful as ever to have him with her. The whole notion that she could ever have done this on her own had been bravado at a time when she didn't think she had a choice. Now they'd spent time together, bonded over the situation, she didn't want to go through any of this without him.

From the moment she'd seen the positive test she hadn't had a choice about being a mother. It was something she would simply have to become. At the back of her mind she had worried she wouldn't be good enough, especially when her role models hadn't been the greatest examples of parenting. Would she love the baby enough when its father had been such a disappointment? If she hadn't got pregnant accidentally, would she even have wanted a family? Now she knew for certain the answer to those questions buzzing around her brain was yes. If she didn't love this baby she wouldn't be so terrified she was going to lose it.

When the pounding sound of her baby's heartbeat filled the room, she heard Niccolo's deep intake of breath before she remembered to take one of her own.

'There we go, baby's heartbeat is strong and loud.'

Gaia wanted to kiss the doctor but was more than happy to have Niccolo's lips on hers instead.

'I told you.' He grinned, and for the first time she saw tears glistening in his eyes too. Perhaps he was invested in this baby more than she'd thought. The idea that there should be two happy parents awaiting the arrival of their first-born had seemed so far out of reach not so long ago. Now Niccolo was showing her that, despite the circumstances, he cared about this baby. Maybe even for her too.

She never could have hoped to have someone not only share this pregnancy with her, but also worry about the baby as much as she did. Niccolo wasn't the biological father but he was showing more concern and interest in her child than Stefan ever had. He was still clutching her hand, proving he was with her every step of the way. She wanted to be cautious about getting carried away, yet with every passing day Niccolo became increasingly important in her life. Captured another piece of her heart. It no longer felt that having a real marriage was merely a fantasy. It was clear he had feelings for her, so it was simply a matter of finding out how deep they ran. Then just maybe she could allow herself to believe they had a chance, a real future together as a family.

Niccolo loved that sound. The quick beat of the baby's heart reverberating around the room was something he could listen to all day, knowing it was evidence that everything was okay. It was proof of that life growing inside Gaia, and as long as they were both safe he would be content. At least for now. He was beginning to see that this marriage of convenience wasn't going to be just a job to him. There were feelings there for Gaia and the baby which he'd let come too far to the surface instead of keeping them at bay as he usually did.

He was supposed to be a fake husband, and a prop dad, but this baby might as well have been his when he was so wrapped up in its development and survival. If he wasn't moved by the situation it would have made him the very monster Christina had told the press he was. He wanted to be a good father, in spite of his own, and he guessed that meant being in touch with his feelings more. It was a relief to know he had them, but also a concerning development for someone who'd tried so hard to protect himself from emotional entanglements in the past. For this fake marriage to work he needed to learn how to separate his feelings for the baby from those he had towards the mother. This baby needed a father to take care of its emotional needs, and to learn from example. The opposite to the upbringing he'd endured with his own father. However, Gaia needed more than another man who would promise her the world and disappear soon after. He didn't want to do what every other male figure had done to her in the past, and if that meant keeping a tighter rein on his admiration for her, then so be it.

'Since you're in your first trimester, you are still in the danger zone. I would advise complete rest. I know it's your honeymoon but you should avoid any further strenuous exercise.' The doctor looked pointedly at Niccolo and he could feel the heat rising to his cheeks, even though he'd done nothing that warranted his embarrassment.

'Of course. I'll look after her, Doctor,' Niccolo assured them both, despite his discomfort. It was only natural that anyone should assume they were any other newlywed couple who didn't stray far from the marital bed. They'd gone to great lengths to make sure no one suspected they were sleeping separately and he would continue to keep up appearances no matter what the circumstances.

'Will I be able to travel back home?' Gaia didn't want any special medical assistance when the time came, making her condition obvious to the world. It was early days in the pregnancy but a scare so soon into their marriage would make it clear she'd been pregnant before the big wedding and give the gossip-mongers a field day. They were waiting to make the announcement after the scan, and the fuss around the wedding had died down. A scandal now would undo their efforts to keep things respectable. The staff here would be discreet if they wanted to keep the royals as guests in the future, but it couldn't be said about every single person they encountered outside of the villa.

'As long as you follow my instructions to take it easy between now and then, and there are no further complications, I don't think that will be a problem,' the doctor told her. 'Now, I'll check in on you again in a day or two, but if you experience any further pain or bleeding don't hesitate to get in touch.' He left his business card on the bedside table, though Gaia was certain Niccolo would have his number memorised already in case something else happened, he'd been so attentive.

'Thank you, Doctor,' both she and Niccolo uttered simultaneously.

'You'll be due your first scan on your return—that should clear any doubts in your mind—but in the meantime...'

'I know, rest.'

Satisfied that the message had got through loud and clear, the medic took his leave, with Niccolo leaving her side long enough to escort him out. He stopped in the doorway to have what seemed to be a very intense chat with her husband before he finally left, with Niccolo looking every bit as serious and intense as he.

'What was all that about?' she quizzed on his return.

'He thought you seemed unduly stressed for someone who's supposed to be relaxing on their honeymoon, but that's my fault.'

Gaia frowned. 'Why on earth would you say that after everything you've done to try and make things better for me?'

As far as she was concerned Niccolo had gone above and beyond his duty as her fake husband, without taking the responsibility of her stress levels upon his shoulders too. Which, without him, would be infinitely higher. If he hadn't stepped up to offer her a way out of her predicament, she would still be trying to think of a way to tell her family she was pregnant and finding it harder to hide it every day. At least that was one problem she'd been able to take care of with Niccolo's help. Now all they had to do was convince the rest of the world they were madly in love to keep up the cover story.

Guilt and shame that the only way she'd got a man to marry her was because a misunderstanding had threatened his career had prevented her from looking at their wedding pics in glossy magazines so far. Another part of her was afraid she'd cry at the images, lamenting the love they were faking for the cameras and in reality would probably never have. For now she'd have to settle for his loyalty and support, which she needed more than ever. It was inconceivable that he could think he was some way to blame for her stress levels when everything which had happened was due to the decisions she'd made. Niccolo had been dragged into her mess through no fault of his own.

He bowed his head before he spoke, as though he was about to confess some terrible deed she was supposed to know about. 'Earlier, in the pool... I know I upset you.'

She was still frowning. 'When?'

He sighed. 'When we were messing around in the pool. I know I crossed the line and that's why you came in here in such a temper. If I hadn't—'

'I didn't come in here because of anything you did. At least not directly.'

Now it was her turn to be embarrassed, having to admit to her own insecurities watching him with other women when she had no right to feel anything about him other than gratitude.

She focused her attention on neatly fixing the bed sheets across her lap rather than looking at him. 'I was…a tad miffed about the attention Cassandra was paying you.'

'Oh?'

She didn't have to elaborate, seeing the moment he realised what she was getting at manifest in a huge grin spreading across his face. 'You were jealous.'

'No. I—er—we're supposed to be married. Are you going to be flirting with every woman you meet? Not that it bothers me, but, you know, the press are never that far away.' She was rambling and not proud of herself for using the paparazzi as an excuse for the way she'd acted, but she couldn't tell him she had feelings for him. It wasn't Niccolo's fault his act of kindness had made this lonely princess fall for him. He shouldn't be condemned to a life of celibacy simply because she didn't want to share him with anyone else. It was none of her business if he wanted to be with someone, as long as he was discreet about it. She didn't have to like it.

Niccolo stood up and for a moment she thought he was going to walk out on her. Instead, he climbed onto the bed beside her. If this was supposed to make her feel less stressed it wasn't working. Her heart was racing and as he took her hand and cradled it in his she was worried she was going to pass out. They'd spent days trying to stay away from one another, and now he was in bed beside her she was worried something was going to give. Probably her heart at the rate it was pumping.

'Gaia, I married you. I know we're not a conventional couple but I've made a commitment to you, and the baby. I'm sorry if I offended you. Yes, I was flattered by Cassandra's not so subtle interest, but I was never going to act on it. I never will.'

'Who's to say you won't meet someone and fall madly in love? What if you want to marry them? Have a family of your own? My father and every man since has abandoned me. The reason I agreed to this marriage was because I thought that couldn't happen again with a man who'd never loved me in the first place.' She hated this neediness in her voice but she wanted to know now, before they got in any deeper, that he wasn't going to break her heart and run off with someone else.

'I don't need to cheat. I have you. I'm not your father or one of your knucklehead exes who didn't realise what he had. I've given you my word I'll stay with you.'

Gaia so desperately wanted to believe that he was going to stay by her side, supporting her, with no desire to find fulfilment elsewhere. Taking care of her the way no one else ever had.

She knew it was a futile exercise but she liked to imagine what it would be like if this was real and Niccolo had feelings for her beyond sympathy or friendship. It was clear he was becoming more to her than a stand-in husband and father to her baby when she was harbouring resentment towards any woman who showed an interest in him. To have a normal relationship with someone who cared for her, who wasn't a narcissistic cheater, didn't seem like such a big ask, but it was all she wanted. More than wealth and status. She'd trade it in for a regular life with Niccolo and the baby if he could ever bring himself to feel the same way about her.

Despite her protestations to the contrary, Niccolo was certain his behaviour had been partly to blame for the sudden decline in Gaia's health. Even if it wasn't down to his actions in the pool, his brief flirtation with the housekeeper had obviously upset her. Finding out she'd been jealous over the exchange had given his ego a boost, but he wanted her to trust him. So he'd told Cassandra to take some time off and had been doing the chores and looking after Gaia's needs himself.

She certainly looked better, her cheeks a little pinker, her smile a little brighter. Niccolo had thought her lethargic since the doctor's visit when she'd slept so much and didn't seem to have the energy to do anything. He supposed perhaps it was the events of the past weeks finally catching up with her and her body demanding she rest. Now she looked much improved for taking the time out.

He on the other hand had worried constantly about her health, and the baby's, and the consequences if anything happened to them. A new experience for him. It was no longer enough to simply be present in a relationship. Gaia needed him to support her, trusted him to take care of her and the baby. It was a huge responsibility for someone who avoided any emotional commitment, but he found himself wanting to please her. Gaia was worth the uncertainty of what exposing these feelings would bring. She deserved so much more than the automaton he'd become to protect himself.

The way Gaia had reacted to his receiving some attention suggested she was jealous. That the spark between them hadn't been imagined and she might have some feelings towards him too. But he didn't want to ask her outright. He could be wrong and risk not only humiliating himself, but also exposing his own growing affection towards her. Worse still, she might admit she wanted a 'proper' relationship and he wasn't sure he was ready to make that sort of commitment. Confessing their feelings for one another might lead to a physical side to their relationship he was trying to avoid. At least by remaining in the dark he wouldn't have to make any sort of decision yet and they could maintain their current status quo.

Regardless of her take on the matter, he wasn't looking for an excuse to get out of the marriage. He'd enjoyed having someone he could relate to, who understood the world he'd been living in, and who was content to simply be with him, looking for nothing in return except loyalty. Something he'd give her until his dying day.

He'd pledged his devotion to her easily because he didn't believe he'd ever find someone who could compare to Gaia. Marriage so far had not been the prison he'd imagined it to be and perhaps that was because their partnership was not a conventional one. Despite his promise to himself to keep her at a distance, he knew he was falling for her more every day. Holding her as she'd fallen asleep that night after her health scare hadn't helped but she made him feel so protective of her, unlike the urge he usually had to get the hell away. He knew he had to open up in order to get her to trust him when everyone else had let her down. Sharing parts of himself he hadn't revealed to anyone before. However, he hadn't expected the floodgates to open and all these other emotions to start running riot. It was one thing to let her see he was capable of being an interested father and supportive father, but quite another to let himself believe they could be a proper, loving family. Thinking they could have everything, be a normal couple, was madness. And all of these worries about her and the baby, how his actions could affect them, and how he had to keep them safe at all costs, made him feel as though everything was spiralling out of control.

Yet he wanted to be there for her and for this marriage to last. As long as he kept those feelings to himself they could have something special. A friendship, companionship, and a partner with whom to raise this baby.

He'd imagined that if he managed his emotions, stuck to the boundaries they'd agreed in this arrangement, that he'd remain in control. Things hadn't quite worked out that way. This attachment he already felt towards something no bigger than a prawn had thrown him for a loop. Surely that worry, that need to get a doctor to Gaia before the worst imaginable thing happened, said that his heart wasn't the desolate wasteland he'd begun to imagine lurked in his chest. Admitting that, however, also brought its own problems. He was in deeper than he'd ever intended.

He didn't want to upset her, especially now he was aware she harboured some feelings towards him too. If they weren't careful they might stumble into a physical relationship, and sex was something he used to avoid emotional ties. Therefore not a step he wanted to take with Gaia when their lives were already so complicated. What they didn't need was to be even more confused about the part they were playing in each other's lives.

He was attracted to her, wanted her more than he'd ever wanted anyone or anything, but he knew he couldn't have her without consequences. Sex in the past had been a means to an end, a physical release as well as a way of avoiding meaningful discussions with his partner. It would be different with Gaia. Exploring a physical side of their relationship moved them into different territory. It would no longer be a marriage only on paper—consummating it would make it somehow more official. Not only that, but it would also bring expectations from Gaia for more from him, and a pressure to be an emotionally present partner. Something he didn't know how to be because he had no experience of it, and no previous desire to be such.

He had to resist that temptation to act on whatever growing attraction was building between them, to focus on Gaia's welfare and the baby's health.

'I've run a nice, relaxing bath for you.' Tomorrow was the last day of their trip and he wanted Gaia to be ready before they undertook that journey back into whatever chaos lay ahead for them.

'Thank you.'

Niccolo helped her into the bathroom, as she was still a little wobbly on her feet. It was a sumptuous tub, most likely installed to accommodate a honeymoon couple, but he'd filled it with bubbles and rose petals instead. There might not be a need for romance, but he reckoned Gaia still deserved some pampering.

'There are fluffy towels and a bathrobe.'

'Niccolo, this is so thoughtful and it smells divine.'

'Don't worry, I know not all essential oils are good to use during pregnancy, but lavender is safe and supposed to help you relax.'

'Thank you so much.'

Happy that she had everything she wanted, he left her alone with the door slightly ajar so that she had her privacy but he could hear if she needed him for anything. Meanwhile he began packing their bags in preparation for tomorrow's departure.

Gaia eventually stepped out into the bedroom dressed only in the fluffy white robe he'd left for her, her skin slightly pink and her wet hair hanging around her shoulders.

'How are you feeling now?'

'Good, thanks. I'm even a little peckish,' she told him, collapsing onto the bed like a fluffy white starfish.

'Funny you should say that…if you're up to it I've prepared a little surprise.'

'Oh?' She immediately sat up again, her interest sparked.

'I had the chef prepare us some dinner. I have a table waiting outside.' Since these things were available to him, he thought he might take advantage every now and then for Gaia's benefit.

'I need to get dressed, do my hair and makeup…' Any trace of the relaxed Gaia disappeared as she stood up, frantically looking for her glad rags.

Niccolo stepped in front of the fitted wardrobe doors and handed her a pair of his jogging bottoms and a black hooded sweatshirt. 'You can wear these. I couldn't find any leisure wear in your wardrobe and I want you to be comfortable.'

'But—but the press…' She looked genuinely

horrified at the thought of being seen in such casual attire and *sans* cosmetics. Niccolo once again felt sorry for her that she never got to simply be 'normal'. There were always such high expectations of her, even from herself, it had to be exhausting.

He pushed the clothes into her hands. 'I've given the staff the night off. The protection officers are sweeping the perimeter, or whatever it is they do to make sure there's no one spying on us. You deserve a night off. I want you just to relax. Okay?'

Gaia took the clothes with a smile. 'Thank you.'

'I'll let you get changed and see you on the beach.' He left her to dress in private before he forgot this was supposed to be about making her comfortable and went to check on their meal outside.

As instructed, the staff had set up a table and two chairs near the edge of the turquoise sea, the pathway from the villa lit with paper lanterns. It was their honeymoon after all and Gaia deserved some romance, even if it wasn't going to lead anywhere. She should feel cosseted at least once in her life.

'Niccolo… I can't believe you did all this.' Gaia wandered barefoot onto the sand, feeling a little self-conscious without her make-up and wearing elasticated trousers and hoodie miles too big for her. It was just as well she didn't have to impress Niccolo because she was not looking her best. He'd made it clear that there was no romantic interest even if his actions suggested differently.

Not only had he been a rock for her during her pregnancy scare, but he'd shown genuine concern for her too. It had been sweet of him to run her a bath, and now this. A handsome man sitting at a table waiting for her as the sun set fire to the ocean behind him was a picture she wanted to remember for ever. It was just a pity the romantic scene wasn't for a real honeymoon.

Niccolo stood when he saw her coming. 'Strictly speaking, I didn't do it.'

'Well, I appreciate the gesture all the same.' He couldn't fool her—it had been his idea and she wouldn't let him deflect the praise. There were very few people in her life who did anything for her out of the goodness of their heart. Usually any sort of gesture was because they wanted something from her in return. Niccolo never asked for anything, seeming only to want her happiness. It was that thoughtfulness which touched her heart even more than a candlelit bath or a beachside dinner.

'I ordered chicken for you. I hope that's all right. I thought you might prefer something plain and I know seafood probably isn't advisable.' He changed the subject back to their dinner, refusing to accept her gratitude. Another sign of a true gentleman who clearly didn't do such things to make himself feel better. Niccolo had a knack of making her feel as though it was all about her, that she was the belle of the ball, despite currently looking as though she'd been shipwrecked.

'Thank you. It looks delicious.' The chicken breast in lemon butter, teamed with herb-seasoned cubes of potato and roasted peppers and tomatoes, tasted every bit as good as it looked.

Niccolo had a seafood platter which he diligently worked his way through, smacking his lips and licking his fingers. It did her the power of good to see him enjoying himself too. She wanted him to be happy, so that being married to her didn't seem like too great a sacrifice of the life he'd been destined to have again with the success of his film.

'This is so perfect I don't even want to think about going home yet,' Gaia sighed as the waves gently splashed onto the golden sand beside them.

'Is it really going to be that bad?'

'It's just the thought of having to put on an act again for everyone else's benefit. I've enjoyed this time away from it all. You know, minus the whole being ill thing.'

'I know what you mean. I suppose I've only myself to blame going into the entertainment industry, whereas you didn't have a say in the matter. It can't have been easy.' He thought of everything he'd gone through in his childhood and how much worse it would have been if he'd had to do it in the spotlight. Two years of damaging publicity seemed little in comparison to the royal family who'd had their doubters even before Gaia's father had been unfaithful to her mother and the country. Not everyone was a fan of the privileged lifestyle afforded to the Benettis through the tax payer, and now he was about to become part of that family, keeping secrets which could bring the whole establishment down if exposed. If he was feeling the pressure he could only imagine how Gaia had coped for all these years before they'd met and she'd been forced to confide in him.

'I didn't know any different to people telling me what to do, how to act, even how to think sometimes. And when my father did what he did, well, I suppose I felt a bit lost. He'd gone against all the rules to simply do what he wanted and it didn't matter who got hurt in the process.' It was clear by the catch in Gaia's voice that she had been deeply wounded by her father's hypocrisy. Not least because the fallout from that had impacted on her current situation, making it impossible for her to admit she was pregnant by someone other than her husband and be seen as having the same 'loose morals'. It wouldn't matter to certain quarters that times had moved on and women could have babies without a man in their lives. He'd understood that enough to marry her.

'Never mind the national implications, it was a lot for you to personally deal with.'

'More than you'd think. I spent my whole life being told by my father I wasn't good enough, a disappointment because I wasn't his son and heir. That women were supposed to be seen, not heard, and just put up with whatever was sent our way. He used to tell my mother she was lucky to even be with him whenever she called him out on his affairs. Yes, affairs, plural. He just happened to make this last one public but everyone has been covering for him for years, because, you know, he was the next in line.' This was the first time Gaia had talked about her family in such a fashion. Until now she'd only talked in hushed tones, afraid anything she said would get back to them. Now it seemed she was opening up, showing him more of the real Gaia. As if he needed to admire her any more.

'Not everyone thinks like that.' He didn't want to be one of those 'not all men' advocates, but it was important for Gaia to realise there were some more enlightened members of society out there, her husband included.

Far from being merely decoration in the background, he thought Gaia one of the bravest, strongest people he'd ever known and her loyalty to her family in the wake of these revelations was even more remarkable.

Her derisive snort, however, disputed it. 'My ex reiterated that idea. He cheated on me too and I thought I should be thankful to even be with him. How stupid was I?'

'You're not stupid, Gaia. Your parents made you think that's what a normal relationship entailed. It's ingrained in us to believe whatever they tell us until we know better.' It was hard not to reach out and hold her when she sounded so alone. It was no wonder she'd got herself into such a mess if she'd been made to believe such nonsense. He could only hope, from the way she was being so open with him, was becoming so emotional about it, that she was beginning to realise how wrong they'd been. She should have been allowed to shine in her own light, not stand in the shadow of the men in her life for the sake of their egos. It made him more determined than ever to protect her.

'What sort of Queen will I ever make, always afraid of what people think of me? Who thinks the only way she'll be accepted is to lie and practically blackmail someone into marrying her?' It was no wonder she wasn't looking forward to going home if she thought she was walking back into the lion's den, but this time she wouldn't be doing it on her own.

'You are loved, Gaia. Not enough people have shown you in your lifetime but I can assure you you'll make a fantastic leader. You've done everything you can to protect your family and the monarchy and I know you'll do the same for your country. As for me…' This time he did reach out, catching her under the chin to tilt her head so she would look at him. 'It was my decision to marry you. One I don't regret.'

The way he was feeling, looking at her now, so vulnerable and fragile, was doing things to him that weren't in keeping with his plan to be the perfect gentleman for her tonight. He needed a distraction.

'May I have this dance?' He got to his feet and held out his hand.

She took it without hesitation. 'You may.'

Niccolo pulled her to him, clutching her close,

and began to sway to the music of the waves. 'I think this is where we came in, isn't it?'

'I think that dance was a little more—er—energetic.'

'I didn't want to get your blood pressure too high.'

'Who knew one dance would cause so much mess? I am sorry, you know, for everything.'

'Hey, I told you before there's no need to apologise. I'm living my best life right now.' He really was. Despite what they had yet to face, he was on a beach dancing with a beautiful princess. Two years ago, he couldn't have believed his life would have had such a turnaround and, though the circumstances weren't ideal, there was nowhere he'd rather be in this moment.

Gaia laughed. 'You mean you wouldn't prefer to be at another glitzy movie premiere with someone who didn't look as though she'd run through a jumble sale?'

'Hey, those are my favourite clothes you're wearing. Besides, you've never looked more beautiful.' He meant every word. With her hair hanging in wet curls around her shoulders, face free of make-up and worry, swamped in shapeless polyester blend, she was stunning. Because this was the real Gaia. She wasn't wearing a mask, or playing a role created by her family circumstances, she was simply a woman dancing barefoot on the sand with him.

Perhaps it was because their bodies were touching, that Gaia had opened up to him, or simply that temptation was becoming too great for him to ignore, but Niccolo couldn't resist any longer. He reached down and pressed his lips gently to hers.

'I think I've wanted to do that from the first moment we met,' he whispered, almost afraid to say it out loud. As though by expressing his feelings he might push her over the edge and ruin this moment.

Gaia lifted her hand and stroked his cheek. 'Me too,' she said softly and kissed him back.

Her soft mouth was his refuge and he found solace there, all the noise in his head quietened by the touch and taste of her on his tongue. Here, now, they were two people enjoying the chemistry they'd never got to explore that first night in the theatre. It wasn't the frenzied passion of a newlywed couple, but a gentle, tentative journey together, getting to know one another. There was no pressure for anything more, even though he wanted it. They both knew that to take this to the next level would be a complication they could do without. It didn't mean Niccolo wasn't yearning to be with her in every way possible.

Gaia's sigh seemed to echo his fear and frustration that one kiss should be all they could afford to indulge. He didn't know what the future held for them as a couple or as part of the wider family other than that it wasn't going to be a smooth transition for either of them. Sharing an innocent kiss seemed to be providing them both with some comfort, so it was enough for now.

She laid her head on his shoulder and let out a yawn.

'I must be losing my touch if I can send you to sleep with one kiss.' He hadn't thought about what would happen once he gave in to temptation but he was pretty sure it wasn't this. It was probably for the best, though, given Gaia's current condition and their already complicated marriage.

'Sorry. It's been a lovely night and I've enjoyed being with you, Niccolo. I'm just so tired.' She yawned again, giving him no choice but to sweep her up in his arms and carry her back to the room.

'You need your rest,' he reasoned when she feebly protested against his chest, telling himself that too when he placed her on the bed and lay down beside her.

'I don't want to go back, Niccolo. I'm scared.' Again she voiced her fears, which were clearly weighing heavily on her mind.

'Of what? You've done the hardest part already.'

They were lying side by side staring into each other's eyes and it dawned on him he'd never felt closer to anyone even though they weren't in a physical relationship. He'd had plenty of those which had lasted longer than the relationship he'd had with Gaia so far, but never had he experienced this overwhelming connection with another person. His heart worked overtime as he began coming to terms with that, and what it would mean for them as a couple. Everything hinged on this marriage lasting, and confessing his true feelings could destroy it all. If she didn't reciprocate, if this apparent infatuation was a flash in the pan, or if she decided she didn't need him in her life further down the line, it was a risky move to show his hand. As always it would be better for him to keep those emotions to himself. He was here to play the role of a supportive husband and father, not take his work home with him. Gaia needed a partner, not another man who'd let her down thinking about his own needs.

Apparently satisfied with his answer, she curled into his side, once more showing the trust she had in him, and seeking comfort from him. He was only too willing to give it.

As much as he wanted to make love to his

wife and show her how much he cared for her, he chose instead to take her in his arms and hold her until she fell soundly asleep.

CHAPTER SEVEN

THE HONEYMOON WAS definitely over. They'd only been back in Lussureggiante for a few days but lying on that bed together, where Niccolo had made her feel so safe, now seemed like a lifetime ago.

There was a knock on the door of their adjacent bedrooms. Since moving into their own residence they'd been doing their best to keep up appearances but he'd insisted on having his own space behind closed doors. A very big flashing neon sign that he regretted that kiss they'd shared before leaving Bali. Gaia couldn't get it out of her head for a different reason: she was falling for her husband.

In an ordinary world that would have been a pre-requisite to their even thinking about getting married, but this was not a typical relationship. It was based on reputation and careers. Emotions weren't in the contract. That was probably why he'd been a bit distant with her since. A kiss became so much more when it was between two people thrown together in difficult and unusual circumstances. Perhaps it was some form of Stockholm syndrome which had prompted the kiss, and for a moment he'd believed he had feelings for someone who was effectively holding him captive in this supposed marriage of convenience. Whatever had led to it, it had become apparent there wasn't going to be a repeat performance. More was the pity.

Another knock.

'Just a second.' She took a moment to check her reflection in the full-length wall mirror before opening the door, flattening down any wayward hairs with her hand and checking there was no lipstick on her teeth. Still wanting to look good for her husband even if it was a wasted effort.

When she opened the barrier between their rooms she was rewarded with his appreciative gaze.

'You look beautiful as always.'

'Thank you.' The compliment lifted her spirit as well as her confidence knowing that Niccolo found her attractive, regardless of the fact that he clearly didn't want to let things between them go beyond a kiss.

'Did you sleep okay?'

'Yes, thanks. The bed is much more comfortable than the couch I spent a week on.' Niccolo's grin didn't quite reach his eyes and she could see that even this arrangement was taking a strain on him.

It was one thing faking a relationship in a villa hundreds of miles away from real life, but quite another doing it back home with the eyes of the world watching them, likely waiting for them to mess up. Living this way wasn't easy, always sneaking around, pretending to be something they weren't—in love. Lying without saying a word. They'd only been married a matter of weeks but she couldn't blame him if he wanted out already. He'd already holed up in a different bedroom, away from the wife he apparently didn't intend kissing.

Today wasn't going to help if he was already having serious doubts about what he'd got himself into when they were going to be spending it together on their first official engagement as a married couple.

'Are you ready, Niccolo?'

He lifted an eyebrow, looked down at his pristine tailored charcoal-grey suit and held up his hands. 'Don't I look ready?'

'You look fantastic, but I meant are you mentally prepared for this?' On the outside he looked like the handsome prince he was now, primed for his adoring public. Inside, if he was anything like her, he'd be dreading taking this show on the road. Although he was clearly a better actor than she would ever make.

He shrugged. 'So far, so good. I mean, I was always going to have to do my royal duty, so I can't complain.'

'I know, but—'

'I've been briefed on royal protocol and etiquette and everything else which could possibly cause embarrassment to the family if I get it wrong.' He put his hands on her shoulders, the first time he'd touched her since that last night of their honeymoon. The weight of his touch was welcome, a reminder that he was there with her even if he seemed further away than ever.

She bit her lip to prevent any further concerns slipping from her lips when it was clear he wasn't going to share any of his thoughts or feelings with her at present. Whether that was down to his wanting to save her from her ever-increasing burden of guilt, or because of those barriers which had been erected between them since their return, she couldn't be sure. All Gaia knew for certain was that they had a job to do today, officially opening the neonatal unit at the local hospital, that they couldn't, and wouldn't, back out of because she had a serious case of stage fright.

'The car is waiting. I suppose we should go. I don't want to keep anyone waiting.'

Niccolo followed her out of the door. 'Do you have a speech prepared?'

'Yes. I worked hard on it, so I hope it comes over okay.' Her stomach somersaulted at the reminder that she would be giving her first public address since the night of the premiere and the ensuing commotion. Although her engagements in the past had been more for appearances' sake, her standing these days carried more weight. If her rise up the royal ranks hadn't garnered more interest she knew her marriage to a movie star would certainly draw a crowd. Niccolo had a lot of fans who would surely take any opportunity to catch a glimpse of him, even if it was at an event for families of premature babies. As the patron for the charity which had raised the money to build the neonatal unit, she had to be there. However, she'd had a sleepless night, anxious about how she and her new husband would be received today.

Being a wife in public was a different role for her from the one she was used to. She would be in the public eye more than ever, with greater expectations now they'd be viewed as a team. He would have his fans who wouldn't think she was good enough for him, whilst there would be many in the upper classes who would look down on him. She couldn't help but think there were many waiting for them to fail as a couple, and in their duties to the country. The extra pressure and responsibility were preparation for her future position as Queen, she supposed. Although, having Niccolo to turn to gave her some comfort. She had him for advice and support, which meant everything, and she felt stronger with him beside her. His encouragement and faith in her actions made her feel more prepared for her position in the family than ever.

As they waited out front for the car to pull around, Niccolo flashed her a smile. 'I'm sure it will. I know you will have put your heart and soul into everything you've written. You're a warm, compassionate woman, which is exactly why they chose you as a representative. Without your support they might not have been able to raise as much money as they did, so I'm sure everyone in attendance will appreciate you being there today.'

'I'm not sure that's true, but thank you.' The black limousine drew up beside them and Gaia was a little calmer as she got in, entirely because of Niccolo. If only she'd had his reassuring influence years ago she might not have made so many mistakes and bad decisions. Unlike her family or past partners, he never made her doubt herself, and always made her believe she was good enough. The exception being that one kiss they'd shared and subsequently never spoken about again. It wasn't his fault she'd read more into it and believed it might have led to something more between them if she hadn't been so exhausted. They'd clearly been clinging to each other for comfort in the moment, and got carried away. That should have been the end of the story, but she hadn't been able to stop thinking about it since and how much she'd like to do it again.

Niccolo could tell Gaia was nervous by the way she was fidgeting with her wedding ring. He could spot her tells which would probably have gone unnoticed by people who didn't know her. On the outside she was a quietly confident figurehead, but he'd seen enough behind the scenes to know that she was also someone in need of support. That was what he was trying to be for her and that meant backing away from the other, less selfless, feelings he was developing towards Gaia.

It had been a mistake to act on them and kiss her, not least because it made him want more. He was afraid that by taking their relationship to the next level it would mean the beginning of the end for them, and he'd promised he'd be there for her and the baby. In the past backing away from his emotions had caused the end of his relationships, but in this case he was doing it to save his marriage. This unfamiliar territory was unsettling for him, a loss of control he'd clung to throughout most of his life.

Ironically being married had made it easier for him to let emotions filter into their relationship. It was a more secure environment, a safe space for him to *feel*, because Gaia had signed a contract to be with him. She wasn't going to leave him broken-hearted and alone, risking the same for herself.

But losing that hold he had on his emotions risked his reverting to that lonely child, vulnerable and hurting. Being a broken version of himself wasn't going to do his career or his wife any good.

He was more use to her as a shoulder to lean on than a partner who would let her down when she expected more from him than he was capable of giving. Survival mode for him, and now for them as a couple, was to lock down his emotions.

This marriage was supposed to be about saving their reputations and providing a stable environment for the baby she was carrying. None of which would benefit from what would probably end up being a short-lived physical relationship if they let things develop.

Which was why he'd moved into a separate

bedroom, away from temptation. If he ended up lying on a bed with Gaia in his arms again it might not stop at a kiss next time.

Niccolo wondered if he should bring up the kiss, explain why he didn't think it was a good idea to follow up on it. Then decided it would probably make things even more awkward between them.

Thankfully the hospital wasn't too far away, so their journey wasn't as torturous as their trip back from their honeymoon had been. Every time they'd brushed against one another they'd leapt back, as if afraid they'd spontaneously combust from the slight contact. They'd needed to get back to the way things had been before their marriage, when all they'd had to worry about was his career, the monarchy and the parentage of her baby. Not potentially falling for his wife and messing things up with his inability and refusal to open up.

Gaia had shared so much with him. Personal details about her life and the way she'd suffered emotionally because of her family and ex-boyfriend, which suggested real trust in him. A lesser person could easily have sold the stories to the press and made a fortune, and she knew that. It said a lot about him that he hadn't been able to do the same in return. She'd bared her soul, but he'd given her scant details about his own life in an attempt to protect himself.

Divulging those secrets he'd held for so long was diving deep into those emotional reserves when he'd been content paddling on the surface so far. Explaining how he'd caused his ex to go to the papers because of his resistance to making an emotional connection risked her seeing him in the same light as Christina did—a soulless monster who didn't deserve sympathy or love. Except there was a part of him that wanted to be honest with her, to show her who he was inside, and stop being afraid of letting himself have feelings for her.

He didn't know if he'd ever have the courage to do that.

In the meantime he needed to focus on something for him outside of the family and away from his wife. He'd been ignoring the calls and messages Ana, and other people from the industry, had been leaving, because he'd been more concerned with Gaia and the baby. This marriage had supposedly been for his benefit too, so perhaps it was time to look after himself. If there were offers out there for him he should investigate because if all of this ended tomorrow he needed his own career to fall back on. He hadn't gone to all this trouble to save his reputation just to throw it away when there were doors opening up for him again. Going back to his job might take his mind off the more…personal aspects of their relationship.

The car stopped and Gaia took a deep inhale of breath.

'Are you sure you want to do this? I mean, it's so soon after your own scare. We can still send our apologies and go home if you don't feel up to it.' Not only was this a highly emotive subject on its own, but she was still in the danger zone when it came to her pregnancy too. Dealing with families of babies born too early might prove too much for her, and apart from anything else she should probably be resting. Niccolo would never tell her what to do but he wanted her to know he was concerned about her.

'I'm a little nervous, but otherwise I'm fine. I think my experience and my current situation will help me empathise with the families. I promise I won't overdo things, but thank you for asking. I don't remember anyone ever telling me I had a choice, so I do appreciate your concern, Niccolo.'

Her smile was dazzling and full of sadness at the same time. He hoped the genuinely happy part of it was for him, and that he hadn't caused her any of the distress her family obviously had. Nor would he in the future. One of their entourage opened the car doors before they could continue the discussion, with Gaia's mind already made up about fulfilling her duty.

They were whisked through the hospital quickly and efficiently with their royal protection officers in tow. It was a totally different experience from the hype and exhibitionism of the wedding, as it should have been. This event wasn't about him or Gaia, it was to acknowledge the work done by the charity, and the families of the young babies who needed that extra support at the beginning of their lives. Yet again, it proved how much Gaia related to her public. She didn't need the fuss or attention to do her duty when she was invested in people.

Jill, the head of the charity, gave a little curtsey as she introduced herself.

'Thank you so much for coming. It means a lot to the charity, and to me personally, to have you here.'

'You're very welcome. I'm honoured to be here to see all the work you're doing.' Gaia shook hands with Jill, as did Niccolo.

Although this was his wife's venture, he was very supportive and proud of her philanthropic endeavours. There were some responsibilities and titles which had been bestowed upon her after her father abandoned his duties, but he knew this was one of the projects close to her heart. Likely even more so now when she was pregnant herself.

'Thank you for coming too, Your Highness. I know some of the nurses here are very keen to meet you.' The twinkle in Jill's eye told him that, although today was about a very serious matter, there was also room for a little fun. This whole royal protocol might be new to him but he had some experience dealing with fans. Schmoosing he could do and feel that he was being of some use today.

'Well, I'm looking forward to meeting your very hard-working medical team too.'

'They'll be very glad to hear it!' Jill led them to the group gathered outside the new NICU, where they received a round of applause.

Gaia approached some of the families who would benefit from the new unit, whilst he went to say hello to the nurses waiting patiently near by.

'Thank you for all the work you're doing here,' he said, shaking hands as he went along the line. It was strange to have people curtseying before him, and his new princely status seemed to demand people keep a respectable distance. In his day job it wasn't unusual to have a scrum of people vying for his attention, grabbing him for selfies on their phones, and thrusting pens at him for autographs. Although he was appreciative of the fans he had, especially after the last couple of years, sometimes they had no respect for his personal space. He wondered if the security guys had a hand in this new dynamic, or if people generally became more deferential when faced with a member of the monarchy.

Certainly, upon his first meeting with Gaia he'd been very aware of acting appropriately in her presence. At first. It was his subsequent lapse into over-familiarity which had caused all the trouble and brought them to where they were now.

Gaia, well-practised in the art of the meet and greet, gradually made her way to the temporary podium, which had been set up for her to give a speech before the official opening. Jill thanked them both again for attending and invited Gaia to address the families and staff in attendance.

While everyone clapped he watched his wife take a deep breath before stepping up to the podium.

'Thank you, Jill, and thank you to the team for inviting my husband and I to officially open this new unit.' At the first public reference to her 'husband', Gaia smiled over at him, much to the delight of her audience, who gave a little cheer.

The acknowledgement and acceptance, both

from Gaia and the assembled crowd, made him stand a little taller, no longer ashamed of the public's perception of him. Even if his current one was based on a lie. But that was the whole motivation behind this sham marriage, though he sometimes seemed to forget that.

'I'm very proud to be patron of this charity,' Gaia went on, 'whose work over the years has culminated in the addition of this state-of-the-art facility for our youngest and most vulnerable members of society. My thanks especially go to Jill and her team, who have tirelessly raised funds in order for this endeavour to finally come to fruition.' She started a round of applause for the team, omitting to mention the work Niccolo knew she'd personally undertaken to secure funding for the project. Not only had she used her personal connections to promote the charity and secure donations, but he happened to know she also made generous financial contributions herself. Anonymously, of course. Gaia didn't do these things for recognition or brownie points, she got involved in important causes because she cared. That was why the way her family treated her at times was so unfair, and why she'd make an excellent monarch.

She finished her speech by outlining the important role this unit would serve to the community, speaking of the lives that would be saved, and concluding that neither she nor the charity would stop their hard work. As long as there were families who needed their support they would keep fund-raising, keep fighting for those precious babies.

The sound of Gaia's voice cracking was lost against the rapturous round of applause, but he'd heard it and seen the quiver of her bottom lip. Niccolo inwardly swore. They'd treated this as simply one of her duties, but, given recent events, it was no wonder her emotions had got the better of her. He instinctively moved closer to her but with a slight, discreet flick of her hand she urged him to stay back. Realising she was right, if he made a fuss it would draw more attention and cause a scene unnecessarily, he stood down and trusted Gaia enough to know her own mind on the matter, but would make sure to give her a cuddle when they were alone again. Yes, he'd been doing his best to limit personal contact but she would need some comforting.

This was a sensitive issue and only days ago they'd feared she might be having a miscarriage. Everything she was hearing today must have been tough when it made her fears a possibility—she could still have a premature baby. She was taking on board the families' stories of their struggles, and sometimes losses, expressing sympathy when she must have been terrified the same might happen to her. The least he could do was put his arms around her when it was all over.

They were given a short tour of the unit, and, though they'd kept a respectable distance from the families and babies using the facilities at present, Niccolo could see the toll the day was taking on her. He waited until they had a moment alone before he mentioned it.

'Are you ready to leave? I think you've done everything you can today and you need to take care of yourself.' He half expected her to deny she was anything but wide awake and firing on all cylinders, so it came as a surprise when she nodded. The jerky motion looked as though her head had become too heavy for her weary body.

He took the initiative by saying goodbye to Jill, then motioned to the security team that they wanted to leave. In seconds they were being whisked back down the corridor, waving their goodbyes to the people who had come out to see them and witness the opening of the new unit.

'Thanks for that,' Gaia said to him as they walked away. 'I think I underestimated the effect today would have on me, and my energy levels don't seem to be as high as usual.' She was almost apologetic for her compassion towards the families, when that was the very reason people warmed to her. Gaia was genuine, she didn't take her responsibilities lightly, or do them for a photo opportunity. Over the course of his career he'd come into contact with many disingenuous characters who portrayed a certain altruistic persona to the world, but behind closed doors showed their true, ugly, narcissistic traits. She was one of the most sincere people he'd ever met, who should be protected at all costs.

'It's an emotional issue, and you're still recovering, don't forget,' he whispered lest anyone should discover their secret. Although they would have to make an announcement soon about the pregnancy when it became too obvious to disguise any longer, and the timing would no doubt cause more speculation, they wanted to wait until they were past the danger period.

She leaned her head on his shoulder for a brief moment. 'Thank you. I can always count on you to make me feel better.'

He wished that was always going to be true but he couldn't make any guarantees for the future. Instead of making promises he couldn't keep he put an arm around her waist and gave her a squeeze of reassurance that he would have her back at least.

As they came to the exit and the security opened the door, they were met with a crowd jostling to get near them, all calling out to Gaia.

'How do you feel about your father having a baby with another woman?'

'Do you have any comment to make on the pregnancy announcement?'

'Will this affect your relationship with your father?'

It soon became apparent that during their time inside the hospital, another scandal had broken and now the paparazzi were scrambling to get her reaction to the news first. Niccolo automatically wrapped his arms around Gaia to try and protect her, whilst security formed a ring around them, forcefully pushing past the reporters and photographers to get to the car.

'Get the door open,' he barked to the burly guard closest to the vehicle.

'Niccolo?' Gaia's fearful plea only made him angrier at the people who had put her in this dangerous position, thinking only of themselves and a scoop, not how terrifying it was to be in the midst of the scrum.

'It's okay. The car's right there, and I'm right here.'

Except just as they reached the door and security made a space for them to get to it, one of the over-zealous reporters managed to grab Gaia by the arm and yank her back into the crowd. She let out a yell as she stumbled back, photographers swarming around her, snapping her distress. Niccolo fought through everyone in his way to reach her, not caring who he shoved aside in the process...all that mattered was getting Gaia to safety. Then he witnessed a paparazzo swing around, his camera bag hitting her in the stomach making her double over, and the red mist descended.

'Everyone, back off! Now!' he yelled, stunning them into silence. Probably because members of the royal family weren't supposed to lose their temper or make a scene, but unlike Gaia's family he cared more about her welfare than appearances.

'You, sort this lot out. Do your jobs.' It was security's turn to take a roasting as he let it be known he was not happy about the way the team had mishandled the whole situation.

Gaia was clutching her stomach and his hand automatically went there too, as if by making contact it would somehow protect the baby more.

'Are you okay?' It was a stupid question when none of this was acceptable, but in his mind her answer was the only important thing in his life right now.

CHAPTER EIGHT

'I JUST WANT to get home,' Gaia gasped, grabbing Niccolo's hand, her lifeline, and let him lead her back to the car through the now slowly dispersing crowd. Her heart was racing like a runaway train, her head spinning from all the pushing and pulling from people trying to get a piece of her. It was only when she was in the car, the door closed tightly against the crowd outside, and she was in Niccolo's arms that she was able to calm down again.

'You're safe now,' he said and kissed the top of her head.

She relaxed into him, his warmth soothing her and making her feel protected.

'W-what happened?' Her teeth were chattering, shock leaving her cold. Niccolo tightened his hold on her, and opened his jacket to envelope her, providing her with more of his much-needed body heat.

'I assume your dear father has caused another

family scandal, dragging you into it in the process.'

She recalled hearing something about a baby but she'd been more concerned with her own when they were getting jostled. 'I wish he would give us some warning before he dropped these bombshells so we could prepare ourselves for the ensuing scramble for information.'

'I think he likes the drama, and attention. It's not fair on you though. How do you feel about him having another family?'

'Honestly? I don't feel anything, not towards my father or the baby. I'm sure my mother will be devastated—it's like rubbing salt in the wound. But when those people swarmed around us, my only concern was for my own unborn child.'

'Mine too, and for you, of course.' He squeezed her a little tighter, as though he wouldn't let go of her ever again. At this moment in time Gaia would be happy to stay here for ever.

Niccolo had been her saviour during the melee. She didn't know what she would have done if he hadn't grabbed her by the hand and faced down those desperate for a story. They'd got what they wanted in the end, pics of the new prince tossing protocol aside to rescue his wife. Her grandfather wouldn't be pleased they'd given the press more fodder for their front pages but none of this was their doing. It was her father who'd caused this. Niccolo had simply been there to catch her again when things threatened to get out of control. He was her rock.

'Thank you for getting me out of there. I just froze.'

'You shouldn't have had to deal with that. This day should have been about the unit and your visit, not having to deal with the aftermath of your father's antics again. And I'll be having a stern talk with the head of security about where the hell they were too.' His voice had a steely edge to it she'd never heard before and she knew he was angry about what they'd gone through. More than that, there was a definite sense of his wanting to protect her and the baby. Everything he'd promised when he'd agreed to marry her.

'As will I. I'm glad you were there anyway.'

'Where else would I be but by my wife's side?'

Gaia knew he was teasing, but within it he spoke the truth. So far he'd been true to his word, supporting her both in her public duty, and in private when things were tough.

'It was easier when it was only the two of us.'

'Was it?'

She wanted to ask him what had changed between them since Bali, but they'd already arrived at the palace.

When the door opened she almost expected to see the red, angry faces of her family waiting to express their disappointment over the latest incident, regardless that none of it was her fault. She'd learned details like that didn't matter. The family reputation was everything. Gaia hoped she would be a more benevolent monarch, and understanding parent. She was still human, capable of making mistakes, and she thought that made her more relatable to the general public. Plus, she hadn't actually done anything wrong. Neither had Niccolo, although the photographs taken at the time might suggest differently as he'd stormed through the crowd to get to her. In her eyes he was the ultimate hero, and she was sure his legion of admirers would feel the same way even if her family didn't.

Thankfully, there was no crowd baying for their blood upon their arrival and she intended on getting to their private rooms as soon as possible. Niccolo disembarked first and reached out his hand to help her out. Except her legs buckled when she made contact with solid ground.

'Sorry,' she said as Niccolo was forced to catch her. 'My legs have turned to jelly.'

'That's the shock.'

She was trying not to catastrophise but she realised now that it could have been much more serious than getting pushed about if he hadn't pulled her from the crowd. After all the stories she'd heard about difficult pregnancies and tiny babies fighting for life, she worried about the little life growing inside her more than ever.

'Are you okay?' Niccolo asked, seeing her hands clutching her bump and mistaking the protective gesture as an indication that something was wrong.

'I'm fine,' she insisted, but clearly he didn't believe her, as he scooped her into his arms and carried her effortlessly up the stairs.

'What are you doing?'

'I'm taking you home.' The possessive, growly tone of his voice made her less inclined to protest, as did the way she was curled up against him. Her face was pressed so close to his neck she could smell his spicy aftershave, feel the rasp of his afternoon stubble against her cheek. Exactly where she wanted to be. Only Niccolo had the ability to make her feel safe, protected, and loved. It might all be fake but for now she needed it, needed him.

Ignoring the stunned reactions as they passed through the house, Gaia enjoyed being the damsel in distress for the short time it took to reach the bedroom. She'd spent her whole life being strong, doing as she was told, and not making a fuss. It was nice to have her feelings validated and accepted. She was tired, frightened, and in need of a little TLC. Luckily her husband was excellent at dispensing it.

'You know we are going to be the talk of the staff after you carried me through the house like a caveman,' she giggled. It wouldn't do their reputation any harm to have people think they were still in the honeymoon stage of their marriage.

'I don't care,' he said, setting her gently on the mattress. 'You're my wife and I want to take care of you.'

He was being so sweet, so tender, it reminded her of that last night on their honeymoon and she couldn't help but wonder why it had all gone wrong between them.

'Niccolo?'

'Hmm?' He was distracted as he pulled back the bedcovers and attempted to tuck her in, but she wasn't too tired to hear an explanation for the emotional distance which had grown between them.

'What happened?'

'It was all a bit of a blur, I suppose. Basically, the papers heard your father got his mistress pregnant and staked us out at the hospital so they could get your reaction to the news first.'

'I meant between us, Niccolo. When you're doing things like this, rescuing me from a crowd and carrying me like Kevin Costner, it makes me think you might actually have feelings for me.' She swallowed down the fear trying to stop her from saying the words out loud and potentially making a fool of herself. It could all be in her head but she found it difficult to believe that kiss and the way he'd defended her today were part of an act.

He let out a sigh. 'Of course I have feelings for you. Do you think I would have risked alienating myself from the press again by shoving them aside if I didn't like you?' Niccolo's admission wasn't the grand declaration she'd been hoping for. Mainly because she'd realised she was in deep herself and wanted him to mirror her feelings to justify them. She'd had too many relationships where she'd been the one who'd loved a lot more than her partner and ended up being the one hurt when it was all over. It would be better to find the truth out now before she caused herself irreparable damage loving someone else who didn't feel the same way.

'Do you kiss everyone you *like*?' She didn't want to sound desperate or needy, but she knew he'd had something of a reputation before their marriage. He'd had a string of beautiful women on his arm before his ex trashed his name, so it wasn't a totally off-the-wall idea. However, they were married, and he didn't seem to do commitment along with romance. The two didn't appear to co-exist in his world, so she needed to know the truth, whatever it was, before it was too late for her fragile heart.

Niccolo thought for a moment, then climbed onto the bed beside her. 'Contrary to popular opinion, no, I don't.'

'So why did you do it, then literally put a wall up between us? Was it that bad?' she joked, hoping it would disguise the hint of desperation she was sure was there in her voice.

Niccolo gave a chuckle. 'No, it wasn't bad. The opposite, in fact, but that's exactly why we can't take things any further. This was supposed to be a no-emotional-strings marriage. That was the only reason I agreed to it.'

'But why would it be so bad for us to admit we have feelings for one another? To act on it? Why are we denying ourselves the chance to be truly happy together?' They were already married, a baby on the way, and to her mind if they loved each other it would be the royal icing on the wedding cake. It was a life, a future, she thought she'd only get to dream about. Her happy-ever-after seemed within reach, if only Niccolo wanted the same things.

'There is no guarantee, Gaia. Especially with

me. I do have feelings for you and trust me, I lie awake at night wishing I could act on them. But it's never going to happen.'

'Why not?' She didn't understand. It was clear there was an attraction, a deeper connection than either of them had anticipated going into this so-called marriage of convenience. So why would exploring those feelings be such a bad idea?

'I'm not good at dealing with my emotions. Strike that,' he said, shaking his head. 'I can't *express* my emotions.'

'That doesn't make any sense, Niccolo. I saw you get angry earlier at the journalists and be tender with me. You express yourself very well when you want to.' Maybe that was the point, he didn't want to have feelings towards her. He was forfeiting his bachelor life to save both of their skins, so it was possible whatever had been simmering away between them was simply a need for physical release and nothing more on his part. At this point in time she was tempted to settle for that if it was all he could offer her. It had to be better than sleeping in separate rooms and thinking he didn't want her at all. A future in bed alone every night seemed very bleak.

He scrubbed his hands over his face, an act of frustration accompanied by another sigh. 'Okay, it's certain emotions I have trouble with.

Why do you think my ex went to the lengths she did to get back at me? I couldn't give her what she wanted—love.'

'It's possible you simply didn't love her; that doesn't mean you have a problem. I mean, her actions did not seem those of a woman you could ever have had a stable relationship with. In my opinion.'

'That's true, but I always bow out before it gets to that stage. This marriage needs to work and I would be risking everything by getting emotionally involved.'

'I'd say it's already too late for that, wouldn't you? It's one thing saying you're keeping an emotional distance but your actions say differently. The way you comforted me when I thought I was losing the baby, the way you swept in today, suggests more than a contractual obligation to me.' She was pushing him, taking a risk that he would admit his feelings for her rather than walk away, and it was taking every ounce of courage she had in her body. Niccolo sounded as though he needed to get to the bottom of this as much as she did in order to move on. She could only hope he took that next step with her and didn't close the door on her for good.

'But it only causes pain,' he spluttered, and

she could see the anguish in his eyes, a trauma hiding in plain sight.

'I know neither of us has been lucky in love but that doesn't mean it can't happen. We have to be open to it at least, bare our scars and hope we don't add to them. Otherwise what else do we have?' This limbo wasn't somewhere she wanted to spend the rest of her life, loving her husband from afar and lamenting their lost chance to have something special. It almost seemed preferable to be on her own than to face that for the duration of their marriage.

'You just don't understand.' He turned away but Gaia wasn't willing to let the shutters come down again.

She placed her hand on his cheek and turned his head to make him look at her. 'Then help me.'

He glanced up at the ceiling and took a deep breath. Gaia held hers, knowing this could be make or break for them, and she wasn't ready to lose the only good thing in her life, besides the baby, any time soon.

That rising tide of anxiety was steadily washing over Niccolo. Even thinking about those bad times made him want to curl up in a ball and block it all out. Just as he had done at the time, his father shouting about how much he wished he'd had a normal son. He knew Gaia's childhood hadn't been a garden party either but he'd never shared the details of his grief with anyone other than a counsellor. It wasn't a time he liked to look back on, or something he was proud of. Gaia would never mock him for how the loss of his mum impacted on him, but she would see him in a different light, she was bound to. To the world he was a confident, motivated celebrity. He'd been strong for Gaia, a rock for her to depend on when things got tough. Once he told her he'd stopped talking after his mother's death, traumatised by the loss, she would only ever see him as weak and pathetic—how his father had described him. Yet he knew if he didn't explain his behaviour now he might lose her for ever anyway.

It was overwhelming as images and feelings stacked up, all vying for space when they'd been denied a place in his head for so long.

'My mum died when I was young. She was my world at the time. There in the mornings to make me pancakes, singing along to the radio, and reading bedtime stories to me at night. Dad was often away "working".' If his father had genuinely been grafting, earning money to support his family instead of sleeping around and making shady deals, he might have understood his absence better.

Niccolo took a moment to check Gaia's re-action, waiting for a sign that this over-sharing was going to do more damage to their relation-ship so he could end this now. However, she was watching him, hanging on his every word and waiting for him to continue.

He inhaled another cleansing breath to take away the bitter feelings towards his father threatening to erupt. This was about Niccolo and his mother, his father merely an incidental character shouting obscenities from the wings and begging for attention he didn't deserve.

'Anyway, I was too young to understand that she was sick. I don't remember anyone sitting me down to explain what was happening. It was all very confusing when she stopped sing-ing, couldn't stand the smell of cooking, and started losing her hair. I know now that it was cancer, that she'd had chemotherapy and that's what had made her so sick, but at the time...'

'The world you knew was different,' Gaia offered.

'Exactly. I thought I'd done something to cause the change and tried to be the best boy I could to make her feel better.' His throat was already raw with the effort of holding back a sob for that child making cold cups of tea and 'Get Well Soon' cards for the only parent who'd ever shown him love. Perhaps his parents had been trying to protect him by keeping her illness from him, but that not knowing what was going on had only made him fret more.

'Oh, Niccolo.' Gaia did the sobbing for him and he had to look away before her tears made him well up too.

'I woke up one morning and she was just gone.' He gasped for air, that overwhelming sense of loss making itself known again, opening up that hole in his heart where his mother had used to reside. 'I wasn't allowed to go to the funeral… I didn't know what had happened. My father just told me she was dead.'

'That's awful.'

'Yeah. It was only as an adult I realised how messed up that was. According to my father I was supposed to just carry on as normal.'

'It's no wonder you have trouble expressing your emotions if that wasn't encouraged, if your feelings weren't validated.'

'I never thought of it that way. I suppose I was just lost without her. I didn't know what to do, or how to act. I shut down and stopped speaking for the longest time. My father's answer to that was to shout and berate me, but when that didn't have the desired effect he eventually took the advice of his new girlfriend, Alice, and arranged for me to see a counsellor. Yeah, he wasn't exactly the grieving widower.' He anticipated Gaia's disgust at the thought of how quickly his father had moved on. That was what had probably irritated him more about Niccolo's grief manifesting the way it had, because it was obvious to everyone he couldn't simply adapt to his new circumstances the way his father wanted. He'd made Niccolo believe it was his fault, that there was something wrong with him when he couldn't forget about his mother and embrace the new family dynamic. Even if Alice had been the first of a string of girlfriends he'd been introduced to and expected to see as a replacement. Fortunately the look of disgust on Gaia's face matched his own current belief that it was his father who'd had something seriously wrong with him.

'You were traumatised, Niccolo. The loss of your mother without explanation must have been a huge shock, you were so young. I'm so sorry you weren't taken care of better.' Gaia tenderly stroked his arm, offering her support, and he grabbed her hand, grounding himself in the present so he didn't get lost in the past.

'I learned it was best for me not to get emotional where relationships are concerned and to lock those feelings away. Then when it inevitably comes to an end I'm capable of functioning again. I don't ever want to be that lonely child, so broken-hearted and lost without the person he loves most in the world he can barely breathe.' It was ironic that he was pouring out all his fears to the woman who could probably do the most damage to him, because it was obvious he had fallen for Gaia. He was clinging on to that last vestige of denial for the sake of his own sanity, aware that when it was gone he'd be vulnerable once more.

'You can't live your whole life afraid of what might happen, Niccolo. We all get hurt sometimes and yes, it's tough and hard to get over, but in the end we all hope to find peace and happiness. You're not giving yourself a chance, shutting everyone out, and letting fear control your life. Don't you want something more?'

He hadn't expected Gaia to understand but neither had he anticipated her helping him see things differently. Perhaps his reaction as a child to the loss of his mother wasn't as extreme as he'd been made to believe. If things had been tackled differently he might have coped with her death better and learned how to deal with his emotions. Instead, he'd been taught to hide them, pretend they didn't exist, and just get on with things.

Now Gaia, who'd been through so much heartache herself, was telling him that it was worth the risk. That he should be willing to chance the pain if it meant someday he would find a person who loved him and would be with him for ever. There was only woman he'd be willing to open himself up for like that and he was in bed with her now.

'Of course I want more. I want you, I want us, but what if things don't work out?'

'Neither of us can predict the future, Niccolo, but you deserve to be happy, to be loved.' She reached out and stroked his cheek with her hand, the soft warmth of her touch a salve to his troubled soul. In that moment it was easy to believe they could have a future together, that it was all there for the taking. All he had to do was be brave.

He leaned in, watching Gaia to make sure this was what she wanted too. When her eyes fluttered shut and she tilted her chin up so her lips could meet his, Niccolo's last defence turned to dust.

Gaia felt as though she was still flying, being whisked through the air in Niccolo's arms, as he kissed her and sent her heart soaring. This was what she wanted, what she'd been waiting for, and it seemed Niccolo had been too. He'd denied them both this chance for something more because he'd been afraid it would mean too much. It was sweet in a way that he liked her so much that he was concerned taking things further would ruin what they had, but she needed this. Needed him.

Niccolo cupped her face in his hands, his kiss passionate and intense. As though by sharing the details of his tragic childhood he'd finally given himself permission to live in the moment. Not get burdened down by catastrophising about the future. And she was benefitting from this new development.

As her fingers moved deftly to open the buttons on his shirt, she knew he needed more than sex too. He'd spent so long keeping everyone at a distance, denying himself any chance of love, he deserved to know what it truly felt like. If their marriage was going to work they both had to be honest, and that started with being true to herself. She knew she loved him, and even if it was too early to tell him in case it frightened him off, she could show him.

Niccolo was nuzzling her neck, his hot breath turning her whole body to one very stimulated erogenous zone. She shuddered with ecstasy as he kissed his way across her collar bone and over every inch of newly exposed skin he uncovered with every button he opened. Her brain was foggy with desire, thinking only about what he was doing to her, how he was making her feel, that she forgot she was supposed to be showing him the time of his life.

As he dipped his tongue into the cleft between her breasts she decided he could wait his turn. After all, they had the rest of their lives to express their feelings for one another.

She'd had a couple of partners, harboured a few crushes in her time, but she didn't remember any man making her as breathless as Niccolo. From the first moment they'd met there'd been a connection, and now as they lay here together in bed it was deeper than ever.

Niccolo stripped away the rest of her clothes, kissing his way along her naked skin, discarding his own clothes in the process. Gaia couldn't wait any longer to be with him, ready in body and soul to take the next step in their relationship.

Breath against breath, eyes locked on one another, they moved together, both seeking that ultimate connection and final release. And when it came, Gaia had tears in her eyes.

'Are you okay?' Niccolo panted, fighting to get his breath back, but clearly concerned for her.

It only made her more tearful. This was the happiest she ever remembered being. When she was with Niccolo she was at peace, no longer doubting herself or her actions, sure of every move. 'I just wish we'd met earlier. That I was having your baby.'

It was the one thing that, no matter how strong their feelings for one another might be, they couldn't change. Although it was what had forced them together so quickly, she didn't think she'd ever stop wishing that part of her life had been different.

Niccolo placed a hand on her belly. 'This is my baby.'

He kissed her tiny bump and the love she'd been afraid to acknowledge for him grew tenfold. She didn't know how she'd got so lucky to meet and marry a man like Niccolo, but now she wanted him for keeps.

CHAPTER NINE

THE NEXT MORNING Niccolo woke up with a smile on his face, seeing Gaia curled up next to him. Yesterday had been a major breakthrough for him emotionally. She'd made him realise that there was room in his life, and in his heart, for love. Perhaps that was why making love to her had been the most incredible thing he'd ever known. He'd finally been able to let down those defences and revel in the feelings he had for her.

There was no point wishing for different circumstances, a chance to erase all of their past pain and heartache when it had brought them here. That wasn't to say he wasn't fantasising that they were in their own apartment in an anonymous life somewhere else. Where going down to the kitchen wearing only his boxers to make her some breakfast wouldn't cause another scandal. Along with getting back into bed and spending the rest of the day showing his wife how much he loved her.

'Morning, beautiful,' he said as she blinked awake.

Gaia smiled and he was sure it was the first time he'd seen her without worry lines etched across her forehead. If this was what made them both truly happy he might barricade them in here for good, away from gossip and lies, and people who would hurt them. Gaia and the baby were his family, finally filling that hole in his heart.

'Morning.' She yawned and sat up, clutching the bed sheet around her body. 'I suppose we should get up and get dressed before people start talking about us.'

'After yesterday I think they already are.' He reminded her of the fracas, only because they'd have to deal with the fallout. Not that he regretted his actions—he'd do it all over again to protect Gaia—but he knew his actions had consequences now. For him and Gaia.

She threw herself back down on the pillows. 'Ugh. Don't remind me. Can't we stay here and have a honeymoon do over?'

Gaia placed her hand on the flat of his chest, and gradually slid it downwards. He groaned.

'It's tempting…' More than tempting, it was literally all that he wanted to do. They'd wasted an opportunity to have quality time together in an exotic, isolated location, instead dodging their growing attraction and letting their personal issues get in the way of their relationship. He would like a chance to have a real honeymoon, to restart their marriage based on love rather than a business deal.

It wasn't something they'd actually discussed. As though admitting they had feelings for one another would ruin what they did have together. After last night he was pretty sure she knew he was in love with her. He'd had to stop denying it himself too when his recent actions around Gaia made it clear he was head over heels for her. Her safety had been uppermost in his mind in the scrum of press yesterday, on top of the pride he'd experienced watching her speech. Knowing his feelings were so wrapped up in hers was what had made last night special, and the world hadn't ended because he'd finally accessed his emotions. If anything, it seemed a much brighter place. He'd tell her in his own time, in his own way, but he wanted to make it special. This change in him, brought about by Gaia, deserved a celebration and he wanted to surprise her with something special to mark the occasion. As soon as he figured out something they could do without an audience.

'Well, then.' Gaia whipped the sheet up over their heads with a giggle so they were enveloped in an Egyptian-cotton cocoon.

He leaned across and dropped a kiss on her still smiling mouth, unable to resist her any longer.

A loud bang on the door soon reminded him that a lie-in wasn't an option, and that they were never alone in this vast building.

'I should have kept my apartment so we could use it for secret rendezvous. Somewhere where we don't have to be anyone but Gaia and Niccolo.'

'It's a nice thought, but there'd probably be a journalist hiding permanently in the bushes somewhere outside.'

'I'm sure we could give them a story to titillate their readers.' He leaned in again for another taste of her sweet lips when the banging on the door sounded again.

'Gaia? Niccolo? Could you please get dressed and come downstairs? We have a lot to discuss.' The sound of Gaia's mother, more disgusted than embarrassed at having to rouse them from the marital bed, soon cooled any ideas of reliving their honeymoon right here.

Gaia groaned and covered her face with her hands. 'Two guesses what this is about.'

'Can't it wait? Do they have a hotline they ring as soon as the sun rises to find out about the latest scandal they're involved in?' He was still getting used to the nuances of being part of the royal family, but this level of accountability made him feel like a little boy again. The idea of his mother-in-law, along with the King, waiting to give him a scolding wasn't something he was looking forward to and there was a chance it could happen on a regular basis when they set such impossible standards.

'Pretty much.' Gaia threw the covers back, the romantic fantasy well and truly over, and sashayed into the en suite bathroom.

Niccolo watched her naked form walk away and restrained himself from following her into the shower. He was in enough trouble already.

They shared a smile and held hands before walking into the lounge.

'Déjà vu,' Gaia whispered, as they found her mother and grandfather sitting there with the morning's papers spread out over the table.

Niccolo held his hand up. 'I know, I know. I should have acted more appropriately but I was concerned for my wife's safety, and the security weren't up to the job—'

'We've let Raimondo go.' The King cut him off with the update.

'Oh. Good.' For someone in such a high-profile security role the beefy guard had been seriously lax in his duty to the future Queen.

'We have more important issues to deal with.

Namely the rumours that Gaia is pregnant.' He pointed to the photographs of Niccolo and Gaia hurrying through the crowd of salivating reporters, both with their hands on her belly.

'She is.'

'I am.'

'But it's the timing, don't you see? People will realise you were pregnant before the wedding.' It was her mother who pointed out the real scandal, at least in her eyes.

'And? We're married. Why would anyone care?' Niccolo was tired of the way they treated Gaia, as though everything she did was wrong. People made mistakes and he knew she had done everything she could to try and fix things. So had he. Now it was about time they were both able to have a bit of peace and get on with their married life.

'We're a traditional family, with traditional values. So are many of the people who live here. This should've been handled differently. We could've said the baby was early...'

'Lie, you mean?' He knew he sounded testy but it was about time someone stuck up for Gaia in the face of her family's constant disparagement.

Gaia placed her hand on his knee, a gesture he took to mean stop talking.

'This isn't how we wanted things to play out

but it's not a crime, Mother. Sex outside of marriage isn't unheard of these days. You both want me to be a figurehead for this country and that means you have to start trusting me. I'm a modern woman and I think most people will relate to me better if I show that. We will put out our own statement announcing the happy occasion once we have the three-month scan and make sure everything is okay. Once the news is out there it should put an end to all the speculation.' Gaia stood to take her leave, and her mother, who looked as if she was going to say something else, seemed to think better of it and closed her mouth again.

The King got up at the same time as Niccolo and put his arm on his granddaughter's shoulder. 'Make sure you run the announcement by our team before it goes public.'

He heard Gaia's sigh of relief as her family made their way out of the room, leaving them to make their own decisions for once. Although he thought she'd handled things with them better this time around. Standing taller and looking stronger than in the first meeting he'd been involved in, she'd been clear that she wanted to do things her own way from now on and would no longer be cowed by their judgement. There was a renewed confidence about her as she'd faced them, an inner strength which was now making itself known on the outside too.

'I think you'll make an excellent Queen, Gaia. Just don't let me down,' her grandfather threw over his shoulder before he exited.

'No pressure, then,' Niccolo whispered to make her laugh and take some of the tension out of the room.

'That actually went better than I expected, considering we're still lying to everyone about the baby's parentage.'

'Hey, it's nothing anyone needs to know. Our business, our family, okay?' Since he'd made the commitment, and subsequently developed feelings for Gaia, as far as he was concerned this baby was his. He was going to be the father figure, and a better one than he'd ever had, if he had his way. Being honest about his emotional problems was the start to a happy life, and he embraced one where he could have a wife and baby to complete the picture.

'I've never stood up to either of them before. I think I've got you to thank for the confidence boost.' Gaia wrapped her arms around him and hugged him hard.

'You just needed someone to believe in you so you could believe in yourself. I'm proud of you. In fact, with this new self-confidence I'm not sure you even need me. I think Princess

Gaia could have raised this baby on her own and been a role model for single mothers everywhere.' It was clear Gaia had the courage and strength to fight her own battles and all she'd needed was a little faith. He considered himself lucky to have been here at the right time, and luckier still that she saw him as more than a get-out-of-jail-free card. If he wasn't convinced she reciprocated what he felt for her he'd walk away and let her flourish on her own. Thankfully, after last night, it was clear there was no need for him to do that. They were both on the same page where this relationship was concerned, and embracing this new start.

'Don't even joke about that. I'm willing to stand up to my family because I have you in my life and I want to protect what we have.' She glared up at him, letting him know in no uncertain terms that she didn't want him going anywhere.

Whilst Niccolo was happy to be the other half of this new royal couple undertaking their public duties, he was also getting antsy about having a project of his own to work on. With the latest publicity, and the numerous messages from his agent to call her, it was clear he was in demand again. Gaia wasn't always going to need him to come to her rescue. When the baby came she might even prefer to take some time out to enjoy simply being a mother. It was important that they both lead fulfilling lives to make this marriage work. He would be a husband to Gaia, a father to the baby, a prince to the country, but he needed something for himself too. It had been agreed during the drawing up of their marriage contract that he wouldn't undertake any work which would negatively affect the family in any way. There hadn't been a clause saying he couldn't work at all. He just had to be careful.

Gaia didn't have to know anything until he found the right project. He didn't want her worrying unnecessarily. In the meantime, he was going to hit up his contacts and see just how in demand a movie-star prince was and what opportunities were waiting for him out there again.

Gaia was on a high as she fixed her hair and reapplied her make-up. She'd been in a hurry this morning to get ready so as not to keep her family waiting. After the talk she'd been rejuvenated, ready to take on the world. She'd started by booking her scan appointment and confirming future engagements for her and Niccolo. They could be a real power couple, using their profile to raise funds and awareness for charity. For the first time she was actually psyched about being in the position she was, where she could really make a difference instead of simply being an ornament.

Until now she'd acted on her family's advice, and that of their advisors. She'd worn what she was told to, behaved how she was told to, went out with men they approved of and represented charities recommended to her. She was beginning to realise her life didn't have to be like that. As Queen she would have some power over her own choices, and she would like to start exercising that right from now on. Not only to get used to making her own decisions, but also so those around her would see she could think for herself, and fully intended to do so. Of course she would take advice on board on certain subjects, but when it came to more personal issues she was going to have her say. She was sure that had a lot to do with Niccolo's support and the fact he allowed her to express her thoughts and feelings without judgement.

'Why don't we go out for something to eat to celebrate my journey towards independence? Or we could order in a takeaway and avoid another free-for-all with the paps. I can't have any champagne but I'd make do with some junk food,' she called from the bathroom. 'Niccolo?'

When she didn't get any response she went

into the bedroom to see if all the excitement, or the exertions from last night, had caught up with him. Instead of finding him curled up asleep on the bed, she saw the room was empty.

The low timbre of Niccolo's voice sounded somewhere below, so she followed it down the stairs to the lounge they'd left earlier. She was about to walk in when she realised he was on the phone to someone. Not wanting to disturb him, she hovered at the door outside, deciding whether to wait there or go back upstairs. She hadn't meant to eavesdrop and it only cast a dark shadow over her mood.

'That sounds great, Ana. I think everything here's under control, so it's about time I got back to work. Yes, I know my popularity is through the roof—why do you think I called you? I've played my role as Prince Charming long enough here and I want to capitalise on that while I can. No, I haven't lost my edge, I'm hungry for something more in life. I've had all of these messages about projects and scripts people want me to take a look at…it's clear that the wedding has restored my reputation. I mean, I don't even know how these people got my contact details, so they're clearly keen. I'm back in the game, baby.' Niccolo's laugh was a horrible mocking sound that brought a swell of nausea from the pit of Gaia's stomach.

She stumbled away, winded as though she'd been roundhouse kicked about the body. Not wishing to be party to the rest of the conversation where he'd no doubt lament his decision to marry her and give up his movie-star status to play this role which he was clearly finding unfulfilling. Worse still, it appeared the marriage she'd begun to believe was real was nothing but a job to him. A means to an end. Now he'd done what he set out to do, regained his reputation and career, there was nothing left for him with her. If showing her love for him by sleeping with him wasn't a reason for him to want to be with her then she had nothing left to offer. There was no reason for him to stay and it sounded as though he was making plans to get away already. She'd been taken in again by a man who was supposed to be there for her, only to leave her alone nursing a broken heart.

The urge to run was all-consuming but there was nowhere to go where she could remain anonymous and weep over the idiot she'd been in private. A photograph of her fleeing the palace in tears was the last thing the family needed. The only place she could go to be alone was her bedroom. No wonder Niccolo found it stifling and couldn't wait to spread his wings again.

She practically fell down onto the bed, her legs no longer able to carry her as the world was ripped from beneath her. Only moments ago she'd truly believed she had it all—a loving husband who supported her, a baby on the way to complete their family, and a real purpose in life. Now she was doubting everything. She'd always believed Niccolo to be a genuine guy and only last night he'd shared some of his innermost secrets, told her he was afraid of losing her. That phone call said different. He was bored, needed a challenge apparently, as though that was all she'd ever been to him. The only thing that had changed between them was the fact they had slept together last night. Perhaps now he'd bedded his princess he'd lost interest.

Even if it wasn't as calculating as that, it appeared she wasn't enough for him. Only weeks into their marriage he was seeking excitement elsewhere. It would only be a matter of time before he cheated on her too. That was what the men in her life always did and she'd been a fool to believe he was any different. The only thing she could do to save herself this time was to take control back and make the first move towards a separation.

In hindsight she'd rushed into this marriage because she was afraid of being on her own, of facing her family and the country as a single parent. Niccolo had offered her a lifeline when she'd been drowning, but now she was head-ing towards the shore perhaps she didn't need to cling on to him so tightly.

They'd both served each other's purpose, his career was apparently on the up again, and she was finally finding her feet and working out her place. It didn't seem fair to keep living this lie. Not if he didn't love her the way she loved him. She couldn't bear to spend the rest of her life feeling that she'd trapped him. It would make both of them miserable and wouldn't be conducive to the happy home she wanted for her baby. Niccolo had no obligation to either of them when it came down to it. Regardless of what he'd said, the things she'd wanted to hear, this wasn't his baby or his responsibility. Very soon she'd be breaking the news to the world about the baby, and she'd already had the conversation with her family. He'd done everything asked of him and now it was time to free him from the contract keeping them together, at least behind closed doors. For both of their sakes. They'd have to keep up outward appearances until the baby was born to give it that legitimacy which had seemed so important at the time, or this aching hole in her chest had all been for nothing.

Niccolo bounded into the bedroom, unable to keep the grin from his face. The phone call to

Ana he'd just finished had proved fruitful, confirming he had offers of work flooding in from all over the world. He'd had to lay it on thick with Ana about his need to get back to work so she didn't think he was focusing on his royal duties instead of his career. Although she'd kept him on her books during the wilderness years, he hadn't been a priority because of the lack of work coming in, and therefore lack of earning potential for her too. He was savvy enough to realise he wasn't anything more than a cash cow at the end of the day, but he needed her too to negotiate these deals. He needed to keep her onside and show that he was ready, willing and able to work, even if he wanted to pick and choose his future roles more carefully. Of course he had different responsibilities and duties now, but he hoped his new status would afford him opportunities which otherwise might have passed him by.

'You won't believe the conversation I just had with my agent...' he started, then he realised Gaia was standing stiffly facing him with a look on her features usually reserved for her family. One that said he wasn't welcome in her room. 'What's wrong?'

'I've been thinking about what you said earlier and you're probably right, I can do this on my own.'

'What?' He laughed, disbelieving that she meant what she was saying. Only a short time ago she'd been clinging on to him, begging him not to leave her.

'We only got married to save face. I was afraid to tell the world about my pregnancy and you needed a career boost. It happened sooner than we envisaged but perhaps that's for the best. At least this way we won't waste too much time trying to force a relationship to work. We don't have to keep pretending.'

'I didn't think we were.' He thought of last night, how amazing they'd been together, and wondered how things had changed so quickly. It was only because he'd been as sure of Gaia's feelings for him as those he had for her that he'd opened up his heart again. Now all of those fears and worries he'd kept locked away for years were unleashed, swarming in the air around him like dark demons ready to steal his new-found happiness and leave him in eternal torment.

'Well, circumstances pushed us together. It was only natural we'd seek comfort in one another but one night together doesn't have to mean for ever. As I reminded my mother, it's not the Dark Ages any more.'

Niccolo was finding it difficult to process the change in Gaia's attitude. Whilst he was happy she had a new confidence in herself, it seemed to have come at his expense. He now appeared to be surplus to requirements. Until this moment he hadn't seen her as someone who would use people and toss them aside once they'd outlived their usefulness. He'd always thought her to be considerate of other people's feelings and someone who wore her own like a badge of honour. All of a sudden she was completely unreadable to him, to the point he didn't know if he'd imagined the look of love in her eyes last night when they'd finally consummated their marriage. Whilst he'd been making plans for a future together as a family, it would seem Gaia had been gearing up to fight for her independence. If only he'd had some warning he might have been able to salvage what was left of his heart.

'What are you saying, Gaia? You want a divorce?' If she was attempting to convince him the feelings they'd shared last night were merely a result of being caught up in this secret about the baby, agreeing to a marriage of convenience that saw them stuck together in confinement, he didn't know where that left them as a couple. It would be impossible to continue on now as though none of it had happened. He couldn't stuff his feelings back in a box and pretend he'd never had them, never shared his deepest thoughts with her because he thought they'd be together for ever. Nor could he imagine a life without her now.

'For the moment I think we should carry on. You do your thing and I'll do mine. When an appropriate amount of time has passed we'll have a legal separation and take it from there. I'm sure you have projects of your own, things you would rather be doing than hanging on my arm.' There was a hardness to her that he'd never seen before. Her jaw was set, her mouth tight, and her arms folded defensively across her chest. For the life of him he couldn't understand the change in her. There was an underlying tone which suggested he was at fault, but all he'd done was support her. If this was her way of saying it was over, that she didn't have any feelings for him, he didn't see any way of fighting it. He couldn't make her love him.

'I was speaking to Ana about an opportunity in Italy—'

'Great. Why don't you go and do that?' She cut him off, not apparently interested in hearing what he was planning, only in getting him to leave.

It was as if last night had never happened. She might regret it, be willing to never think about it again, but unfortunately he would remember every second of it until the day he died.

'Have I done something wrong? I thought we were really at the beginning of something special.'

'You played the role perfectly, Niccolo. Now it's time to move on to the next one.' She gave him a smile that better suited one of those shop greeters who told you to have a nice day and deep down didn't care if you got hit by a bus once you left the store. They were just words, with no emotion behind them. Almost as though she'd become the sort of automaton her family wanted to smile and wave and not rock the boat. This wasn't his Gaia, and she was making it clear she never had been.

'What about the baby?' A big part of the marriage deal had been to provide security for the baby. The idea of going back to separate lives now was stealing that future family away from him and the child.

He was invested in them as a couple, and as a result of that had finally embraced the possibility of his becoming a father. It was a chance for him to be that loving parent he'd had and lost, and to be better than his own father in the process. He hoped he'd be the kind of dad to listen to his son or daughter and encourage them to express how they felt. Not inflict the kind of emotional trauma his father had put him through which had followed him into adulthood and wrecked every relationship he'd ever had. It was ironic that, just when he'd learned to let himself love, Gaia revealed she didn't need him. He might have been better off keeping his feelings on lockdown for a bit longer. Then he wouldn't have had his heart ripped out of his chest finding out their marriage was over, that Gaia didn't love him back. The only consolation he had was that he hadn't spilled his guts out to her, confessing his love and furthering his humiliation. Although discovering she didn't love him was a small, unwanted, badly wrapped gift.

Going back to his day job would give him an interest away from the royal duties, but it was no longer his entire life. Being with Gaia, planning a future around the baby, had given his existence a different depth, given it more meaning. Without them again he didn't know who he was any more.

'We'll be fine without you, as I'm sure you will be without us,' she said, her insistence inflicting further injury, as though she'd just drop-kicked his freshly plucked heart.

He thought he saw her smile waver, then put it down to wishful thinking when she was still staring, waiting for him to leave.

'You want me to go now?' he asked, incredulous that this should be over so quickly without prior warning. Though he supposed it was in keeping with the nature of their marriage—hasty, ill thought-out, and something which was going to be difficult to explain. What could he do but bow out if that was what Gaia truly wanted? He did have some options he wanted to explore work-wise—perhaps that would give him some space to think about what had happened, maybe figure out what had gone wrong. Hopefully it would keep him busy enough to distract him from the massive void Gaia would leave in his life. He wasn't going to have much of a career if he reverted to that traumatised boy who couldn't find the words to express the emptiness left behind after the loss of his loved one. Not unless they brought back silent movies.

'I think it's for the best. You've fulfilled your side of the bargain, so now I'm setting you free.'

It was on the tip of his tongue to tell her he didn't want to go, that this was more than a business arrangement and she wasn't doing him any favours. But he saw the steely determination in her eyes and knew it was no use arguing with her. Gaia had made up her mind to go it alone after all. He just wished she'd done that before he'd fallen in love with her.

* * *

'Don't you think you should answer that?' Gaia's mother nodded towards the phone buzzing in her hand.

'No. He'll have to give up eventually.' She'd turned off the sound but Niccolo was persistent. Her voicemail was full with messages he'd left but she hadn't been able to bring herself to listen to them. It had been difficult enough sending him away without hearing his voice again, reminding her of what she'd lost. He might have said it was her who'd thrown away their marriage, but he'd thank her when he had his own life back.

If he'd had so many great opportunities thrown his way she didn't want to hold him back any more.

As much as she wanted the sort of man who'd agree to marry her to save her reputation, she needed it to come from love, not obligation. Somewhere along the way they'd confused the two. Or at least she'd been acting out of love and he'd been a slave to obligation. Either way, it hadn't been fair to carry on the way they were. It was clear to her she'd fallen in love with him, or hearing him tell his agent that being with her had just been a job to him wouldn't have hurt so much. To her, sleeping together had been a culmination of their love, but apparently to him it was still all part of the act. One which he should have won awards for when he'd convinced her he had real feelings for her. It wouldn't have been any life for her, or the baby, trying to convince herself that it was better to have a husband at least in name rather than doing this on her own. She'd realised too late that she did need love, that a marriage of convenience wasn't enough for her. By that time she'd already given her heart away again, but at least by calling things off herself she'd clung on to a little dignity.

It was thanks to him that she had found her self-confidence again and it was that inner strength she was going to dig deep into to see her through the rest of this pregnancy and beyond.

Although since Niccolo's departure her mother had been surprisingly supportive, even coming with her today for the first scan. Still, Gaia had opted not to inform her of the real reason they had split, only telling her that things hadn't worked out.

'I'm not so sure,' her mother said as her phone renewed the incessant buzzing.

In the end Gaia had to turn it off altogether. It was torture knowing that Niccolo wanted to speak to her, but also being aware it wasn't going to achieve anything. Eventually he'd realise he was off the hook and find joy in the things he really loved.

'I'm not giving him any choice.' She threw the phone into her bag so she wouldn't even have to look at it, lest she was tempted to listen to what he had to say and give in to the easier life he was likely offering. It seemed taking the higher ground came at a cost, but she hoped it would be worth it in the end. If nothing else she could teach her child that appearances weren't everything, so this toxic legacy wouldn't continue into another generation. Whilst being part of the royal family dictated decorum and responsibility, it shouldn't mean lying and faking a life that suited a narrative from hundreds of years ago. People fell in and out of love, made mistakes, and got pregnant outside of marriage. They shouldn't be forced into marriage to save face. Perhaps if someone had ended this cycle of deceit her father wouldn't have acted the way he had, and she would have been strong enough to stand on her own. There would have been no need to drag Niccolo into their dysfunctional family.

'Are you going to tell me what happened? I mean, I know the wedding was a rush but I thought you genuinely loved each other. At the end of the day that's all that matters.' Her mother apparently wasn't going to let the matter drop so easily. The split must have come as a shock to her when they'd initially been so gung-ho about getting married in the first place.

Gaia thought about the lies her father had told, the life her mother had been forced to live, and knew it wasn't fair to keep her in the dark any more. What did it matter now that she and Niccolo weren't together anyway?

'The baby isn't his. I mean, he knew that, it's not why we split up. He only agreed to this to save our reputations. Genuinely nothing had happened between us when those photographs were taken, but I knew how everyone would react when they found out I was pregnant.'

'He married you anyway?'

'Yes, well, he's a good man. He knew how bad it would look for me…and him, I suppose. People would've assumed he was the baby's father no matter what we said. We thought a marriage would save both of our reputations, and his career had been in freefall up until the premiere.'

'Okay, so it was a marriage of convenience. That's not unheard of…this family has been doing it for years.'

Gaia was powerless to prevent her eyebrows almost disappearing into her hairline. 'You and Dad?'

It would explain a lot about her father's behaviour if he'd been coerced into a marriage he hadn't wanted, even if it didn't excuse it.

Her mother nodded. 'Although I'm not royalty, as your father liked to point out on a regular basis, I was from the *right* family. We had connections which opened up some very important financial avenues and helped strengthen economic relations with other countries. Your father had a lot of side-interests.'

The double meaning wasn't lost on Gaia when his infidelity had turned out to be as prolific as the international duties he carried out.

'I had no idea. I assumed you'd been in love once.'

'Well, one of us was. I'm not sure your father truly loved anyone more than himself.' She gave a half-smile which only served to make her look even sadder than usual when she talked about Gaia's father.

'I'm so sorry, Mum. You always deserved so much better. But it does prove to me that I made the right decision in telling him to leave.'

'Why's that?'

'Unrequited love in a marriage is never a good thing.'

'Oh, Gaia.'

She found herself swamped in a tight hug, her mother's embrace something she hadn't experienced in a long time.

'It's all right, I've realised I'm stronger than I knew. I mean, that might have had something to do with Niccolo too, but I think I'll be all right. I have the baby to think about and that's more important than a silly crush.'

'He's really not coming back?' her mother said softly, yet the words hit hard, causing tears to mist Gaia's vision.

She shook her head, dislodging a solitary tear rebelling against her refusal to cry any more over the loss of her fake husband. 'I didn't think it was fair on either of us to make him stay. It's not his fault I fell in love with him and he doesn't feel the same way.'

'Did you even give him a chance to have his say?'

'I overheard him on the phone to his agent. Apparently he's highly in demand now that he's a movie-star prince. Reading between the lines, he was stifled here. I didn't want him to get bored and end up cheating on me. For him to take work and simply never come back would almost be worse than never loving me.'

'It is,' her mother said, wiping away the tears that were now flowing freely with her handkerchief. 'I'm sorry we put so much pressure on you that you thought marriage was the only way out. What about the father—is he completely off the scene?'

'Yes. Niccolo was the only man I thought would be a good dad, but parenthood shouldn't be forced on someone any more than marriage should. I was asking too much from him.'

'But he was willing to do it, Gaia. Are you sure there's no way forward? If marrying you and being father to your baby so people won't think badly of you doesn't say love, I don't know what does.'

'I told you, he's a good man,' Gaia huffed, put out that her mother seemed to be on his side. She'd been through all of this in her own marriage and knew how it panned out. If anything she should be applauding her for pre-empting the inevitable heartbreak and taking control now before another child was born into a one-sided relationship. So it didn't grow up thinking it wasn't worthy of love too.

'I saw the way he looked at you, Gaia. I think it was more than that. Don't let the toxic relationship I had with your father cloud your judgement. If he had ever looked at me the way Niccolo looks at you we would never have had a problem. Niccolo loves you.'

Gaia thought of everything he'd done for her and how amazing last night had been. As good an actor as he was, she didn't think he could have faked all of that, but it was clear that the resurgence in his career was a big deal to him. He'd risked it to help her and now this was her way of paying him back. Giving him his life again instead of forcing him into her world. Yet there was a selfish part of her wishing he'd fought harder and hadn't got on the plane. That he was here with her to see their baby.

'If he really loved me, he wouldn't have gone.'

Her mother threw her hands up. 'You've probably confused him about what it is you do want. I'm not sure I know any more.'

'Right now I want to know the baby is all right.' The truth was she wanted it all—Niccolo, the baby, and a happy family—but life had taught her that it wasn't possible and she'd be a fool to believe otherwise.

The sonographer came in at that moment and positioned herself in front of a screen. 'Okay, Your Highness, if you could lift your top up I'm going to put some gel on your belly.'

Gaia complied, wincing when the cold substance made contact with her skin.

'Sorry about that, it's just to help the Doppler move over your bump. Not that you have much of one at this stage.' The woman sounded nervous, something Gaia was used to. People often got a tad tongue-tied when they met a member of the royal family. On this occasion, however, it wasn't doing anything to ease her own apprehension. She would have preferred to have a pronounced pregnancy belly at this stage to put her mind at rest that the baby hadn't been adversely affected by everything that had gone on lately.

'I had a bit of a scare recently. Some cramps and sickness. It's been a stressful time.'

'I saw that in your notes but the attending doctor reported a strong heartbeat. We'll check now to put your mind at ease.' If the woman had put two and two together over the dates and realised Gaia was pregnant before the honeymoon she didn't give any indication. The private hospital was used by the entire royal family and their discretion could be counted on. One less thing she had to worry about.

Gaia held her breath waiting for that tell-tale sound again, her eyes locked on the screen in anticipation of seeing that tiny bean which had caused so much trouble. The only thing keeping her going in the wake of her all-encompassing heartache.

It seemed like for ever before the woman spoke again. Even Gaia's mother seemed to be agitated, standing up to peer at the screen herself, as though she'd be able to spot something before the trained medical staff.

'Is everything all right?' Gaia finally asked, unable to bear the silence and uncertainty.

'I'm just having trouble finding baby...'

It was enough to tip Gaia over the edge. She was wrong, she didn't want to do this alone.

'I want Niccolo,' she sobbed.

Her mother took her hand and squeezed.

The sonographer moved the Doppler device with a renewed determination.

Then the door burst open and Gaia was glad she was lying on a hospital bed because she was sure she would have collapsed when she saw who'd walked in.

'Gaia? What's wrong? Why wouldn't you answer my calls?' Niccolo flew to her side and she could tell immediately by his stubble and the rings under his eyes that he hadn't been sleeping any better than she had in the few days since they'd separated.

'Niccolo? What are you doing here?'

Her mother moved so he could get to the side of the bed, leaving go of her hand so Niccolo could take it in his. It didn't matter how they'd parted, in that moment she needed him here with her.

'I knew it was the scan today. I had to be here, even if you don't want me—'

'There we go. Baby was just playing hide and seek with us.' The sonographer interrupted them with the good news before Gaia had the chance to tell Niccolo that she had wanted him here.

'Can we see?' Niccolo asked, squeezing her hand tight as the sonographer turned the screen for them to see the grainy black and white image, the tiny figure floating in the middle.

'Everything's all right?' She needed confirmation before she'd let herself believe it and get too carried away with the thought that it might all just work out. The fact that Niccolo had come back for the scan, for a baby that wasn't his, gave her a flutter of hope that all wasn't lost.

'Baby seems perfectly happy and well. I'll print out the pictures for you, then I'll give you a bit of time to get cleaned up in private.'

Gaia took hold of the precious pictures of her baby and kissed them.

'I'll give you some privacy too. You have things to discuss,' her mother said, leaving the room with the sonographer so Gaia and Niccolo were alone.

Now was the time for honesty for both of them, it was make or break, but Gaia was afraid by telling him she loved him she was losing the control she had over the situation. She was risking leaving herself open to feeling unwanted again if he told her he didn't feel the same way.

* * *

'I'm glad the baby's okay,' he said, unsure of what he was doing here. Gaia had sent him away less than a week ago, telling him she didn't want him, and she'd proved her point since, refusing to take his calls or messages. Yet he hadn't been able to give up on her, or them. Perhaps it was the idea that a family was almost within his grasp because he couldn't believe she didn't love him. It wasn't that he was so conceited he didn't think it a possibility. Rather, he'd spent the last nights analysing their every moment together. He'd worked with the best actors and Gaia would be award-winning if it turned out this was still just a business deal to her.

The way she fitted in his arms so perfectly and readily, the plans they'd had for their family, and the love they'd made so tenderly, said they shared something deeper than necessity. Whilst they might have started out in a marriage of convenience, he'd fallen in love with Gaia. He was a different man to the one she'd married, no longer content to hide away from his feelings. Now he was back to make sure she wasn't making the same mistakes he had in the past.

'Why did you come back, Niccolo?' Her voice

was barely a whisper, as though she was afraid of the answer.

'For you, for the baby, for us. Things ended so abruptly I wanted a chance to talk things through properly. To tell you I love you in case you were in any doubt.' It had occurred to him on those lonely nights wondering what he'd done wrong that he'd never told her how he felt. That she might have believed he'd only used her for sex when that night together had been his way of showing her how he felt, even if he hadn't been able to express it in words. The idea of losing her for ever had given him the courage to actually tell her.

'You—you love me?'

'Yes. Is that so hard to believe?' He smiled, hoping to charm her back into his life.

'It's…unexpected.'

'So, you see, I didn't have to leave. I just need to know if you feel the same way, then we can be together as a proper family.'

Gaia shook her head as if she was trying to dislodge that thought. 'It doesn't change anything. You'll tire of us. It would only be delaying the inevitable if you came back.'

Niccolo laughed because she was being completely unreasonable as far as he could see. She wasn't saying she didn't love him, but she was afraid to in case things didn't work out. In some ways he could relate. After all, that was how he'd operated in all of his relationships until he'd met Gaia and had to confront the fact that he wanted to be with her.

'Gaia, we can't live our lives being afraid to take a chance on love. Isn't that what you told me? What makes you think that I would ever tire of being with you when I clearly can't live without you?'

'I heard you on the phone to your agent saying this life wasn't enough. That you were excited about the new job opportunities being offered to you. And don't forget, you went. You didn't even fight for us.'

There was so much to unpack in that statement it took Niccolo a moment to figure out what had happened.

'For a start, you asked me to leave. I thought if you didn't love me that there was no point staying here and upsetting you. As for the phone call, yes, I was thrilled to hear people wanted to work with me but not for the reasons you think. I'm part of this family, of course I'm going to do my duty, but that doesn't mean I'm limited to cutting ribbons and waving at people, does it?'

She opened her mouth to answer but he carried on because he had a lot to say. He was done with everyone thinking badly of him when he'd done nothing to deserve it. Gaia of all people should have realised he wouldn't shirk responsibility.

'I know as a member of the royal family my day job is supposed to take a back seat. I agreed to that when I signed those papers before the wedding. And, to be honest, I didn't think it would be much of a problem when I was still trying to rebuild my reputation. Then Ana started calling to let me know there was a chance for me to still be involved in the industry as a mentor and a patron to a charity for aspiring actors and directors. I thought it was a good opportunity to prove my worth in the family, to show I'm committed to my new role. I went because I wanted you to see I'm not going to be living off your coat-tails for the rest of my days. I intend to earn my keep, and people's respect, on my own merits. And I want our children to grow up being proud of us both and knowing they can make a difference in the world, not simply decorate it.'

Gaia couldn't process everything he was saying, so she focused on that last part promising them a future together. 'Our children?'

'Yeah, well, if we don't completely mess this

one up, I thought we might want to extend the family.'

'That sounds nice. Really nice.' After his declaration of love, turning up for the scan, and explaining why he'd been so excited about the prospect of work, Gaia was beginning to let herself imagine their life together again. One without secrets.

'So…does that mean you'll take me back?'

She thought about the life she would have without him in it and it was nothing compared to the one he was offering her now, if she was willing to give him a chance and believe he was different to all the other men she'd had in her life.

'Yes, Niccolo, I want you in our lives.' She placed his hand on top of her belly and hoped their baby would grow up in the safe, loving environment it deserved.

'In that case, Your Highness,' he got down on one knee beside the bed and Gaia had to peer over to see him, 'will you do me the honour of becoming my wife for real? Will you marry me again?'

'I will. I love you, Niccolo,' she said, throwing her arms around him when he stood up again.

The kiss they shared, as two people finally honest about their feelings, was so full of love and a need to make one another happy she thought her heart would burst.

The Princess had her fairy-tale ending after all.

EPILOGUE

Four years later

'EMILIA, WAVE AT the crowd.' Gaia encouraged her daughter to make her presence known on the balcony with the rest of the royal family even though she could scarcely see above it, aware that the throng of people lining the streets would want to see her.

Although she was fiercely protective of her family, on occasions such as the diamond anniversary of the King's coronation they were expected to have a visible presence.

'Do you want me to take Leo?' Niccolo asked.

She nodded and extricated her exuberant toddler from his koala position on her waist. Little Leonardo was too young to understand what all the fuss and noise was about, and once he'd given everyone the photo op they'd been waiting for she would take him back inside the palace.

They were lucky to live away from the city

these days. Once Emilia had been born they'd made the decision to live in one of the other royal residences in the countryside to afford them more privacy. It was smaller than the palace but had become their family home, where she and Niccolo had been able to live a relatively normal life. They'd even renewed their vows in the grounds and Emilia had been delighted to be a flower girl on the day, only witnessed and attended by Gaia's mother and grandfather. That was how they lived their lives these days, out of the spotlight as much as possible.

They carried out their duties as members of the royal family as usual but didn't parade their children in front of the cameras. It was important to her and Niccolo that they had as normal a childhood as possible, not under constant scrutiny as she had been.

'I can put them to bed if you want to stay and watch the show,' Niccolo told her as they watched the stage opposite the palace filling with the latest chart singers, keen to celebrate the King's anniversary in front of the packed crowd.

'That would be great. I'll stay for a while, then you can come out if you want.' They had a nanny to help out when they were required at state functions and public engagements, but they preferred to spend time with their children. Niccolo was an excellent father. He'd worried he wouldn't be able to show those emotions which had caused him so much trouble in the past, but he needn't have worried. The moment Emilia was born he burst into tears, the same when his son was born a year later. He loved nothing more than reading them bedtime stories or playing hide-and-seek in the grounds with them. There wasn't a day that went past without him hugging his children, and his wife, and telling them how much he loved them.

Gaia loved being a mother, and being married to Niccolo. She had so much unconditional love in her life now the happiness had pushed out those negative feelings about herself and her family. Life was too short not to enjoy the precious time she had with her husband and children.

They had their own charitable arms—she worked with many mother and baby groups, and Niccolo had his mentorship with aspiring actors and directors. It gave them some time apart and something to talk to each other about when they were reunited. Those separate interests gave them a life beyond the palace walls and also made them look forward to seeing one another again at the end of the day. They had the best of both worlds.

'Okay, kids, let's go. Wave goodbye.' Niccolo

waited until the children gave the crowd what they'd come for, then dropped a kiss on Gaia's lips. Even now he was able to excite her whole body with one slight touch.

The sound of wolf whistles and flash of cameras reminded them that they'd just given a very public display of affection, but her mother and grandfather didn't bat an eyelid in their direction. They were popular now because of Gaia and Niccolo's relationship and the new generation of the family. It had taken some time but her grandfather had begun to realise some of those traditions had kept them at a distance from the rest of the country, and showing they were human after all had helped people warm to them more. They had taken some flak announcing the first baby when it was clear she'd been pregnant before the wedding. Mostly, though, people had accepted she was human and made mistakes like everyone else. Not that she thought of Emilia as a mistake when it was her who'd brought Niccolo into their lives in the first place.

'I'll be in soon,' she told Niccolo and he gave her a wink before leading the children inside. They were sleeping in the guest room in the palace tonight, with Gaia and Niccolo in the adjoining room he'd once slept in alone. As she watched him walk away looking so handsome in his navy tailored suit she decided she wouldn't stay at the party for too long.

One day she would be expected to rule the country and assume all the responsibilities her grandfather currently undertook. Until then she would spend every second she could with her husband and any dancing they did now was in private.

From now on Niccolo Pernici's moves were reserved solely for her.

* * * * *

If you enjoyed this story, check out these other great reads from Karin Baine

Falling Again for the Surgeon
Single Dad for the Heart Doctor
Festive Fling to Forever
A GP to Steal His Heart

All available now!